A few moments after I sat down, the glass in the window beside me *creaked* as if something more material than the wind were pressing against the pane. I stared unseeingly at the book in my hands, and tried not to look at the window when it began to rattle violently, as if someone were growing impatient.

I couldn't focus on the print anymore, and I glanced about the room as the rattling increased. It occurred to me that while I had been warned not to look *out* of the window, I could safely let my eyes just *slide* across it.

I turned my head. . . . It was about two feet outside the window—a face or mask or muzzle of a more gleaming black than the darkness around it. A pitiless, hopeless man-animal face alive with knowledge but dead with a monstrous melancholy and a monstrous malice. There was the sheen of needlelike white teeth. There was the dull pulsing glow of eyes like red coals that grew larger as it approached the window.

The lights all went out. . . .

From THE OLDEST SOLDIER

# THE MIND SPIDER
## AND
## OTHER STORIES

## BY
## FRITZ LEIBER

ace books

A Division of Grosset & Dunlap, Inc.
1120 Avenue of the Americas
New York, New York 10036

CONTENTS

# FOREWORD

Years ago my window at the University of Chicago overlooked the west stands of Stagg Field. One evening I watched a lightning storm playing over the Loop.

Nature was badly off key that night. The thunder didn't rumble or roar. It *screamed* faintly, four seconds after each flash. I remember thinking that if lightning could twang the rails of Chicago's elevated tracks they might make such a sound. Several other persons heard it and shivered as I did.

Ten years later electronic experts discovered that on rare occasions lightning generates a radio signal which circles the earth and returns to its point of origin as an audible whistle. Maybe that was my scream.

But also ten years later there was built below the west stands of Stagg Field the graphite-dark atomic furnace that first released on earth the energy of the suns. Maybe the molecules felt *that* coming and screamed a warning.

Either way it's a weird and wonderful world. Just consider: an infinite universe . . . stars that are living hydrogen bombs . . . trillions of atomic worlds in a grain of dust . . . jungles in a drop of water . . . black gulfs of space around each planet . . . black Freudian forests around each conscious mind—you know, I sometimes think the powers that created the universe were chiefly interested in maximizing its mystery.

That's why I write science fiction.

—FRITZ LEIBER

# THE HAUNTED FUTURE

*My strangest case, bar none, from the Psychotic Years
was the Green Demon of New Angeles.*
      —from the notebooks of Andreas Snowden

It would be hard to imagine a more peaceful and reassuring spot, a spot less likely to harbor or attract horrors, even in America of the tranquil Early Twenty-first
Century, than the suburb—exurb, rather—of Civil Service
Knolls. Cozy was the word for the place—a loose assembly of a half thousand homes snuggling down in the warm
moonlight a mountain ridge away from the metropolis
of New Angeles. With their fashionably rounded roofs the
individual houses looked rather like giant mushrooms
among the noble trees. They were like mushrooms too in
the way they grew with the families they housed—one
story for the newlyweds, two for the properly childrened
and community-seasoned, three for those punchdrunk with
reproduction and happy living. From under their eaves
spilled soft yellow light of the exact shade that color an-
alysts had pronounced most homelike.

There were no streets or roads, only the dark pine-
scented asphalt disks of sideyard landing spots now hold-

ing the strange-vaned shapes of 'copters and flutteryplanes locked for the night, like sleeping dragonflies and moths. While for the ground-minded there was the unobtrusive subway entrance. Even the groceries came by underground tube straight to the kitchen in response to the housewife's morning dialing, delivery having at last gone underground with the other utilities. Well-chewed garbage vanished down rust-proof ducts in the close company of well-bred bacteria. There were not even any unsightly dirt paths worn in the thick springy lawns—the family hypnotherapist had implanted in the mind of every resident, each last baldie and toddler, the suggestion that pedestrians vary their routes and keep their steps light and rather few.

No night clubs, no bars, no feelie pads, no mess parlors, no bongo haunts, no jukebox joints, no hamburg havens, no newstands, no comic books, no smellorama, no hot-rods, no weed, no jazz, no gin.

Yes, tranquil, secure and cozy were all good words for Civil Service Knolls—a sylvan monument to sane, civilized, progressive attitudes.

Yet fear was about to swoop there just the same. Not fear of war, missile-atomic or otherwise—the Cold Truce with Communism was a good fifty years old. Not fear of physical disease or any crippling organic infirmity—such ills were close to the vanishing point and even funerals and deaths—again with the vital aid of the family hypnotherapist—were rather pleasant or at least reassuring occasions for the survivors. No, the fear that was about to infiltrate Civil Service Knolls was of the sort that must be called nameless.

A householder crossing a stretch of open turf as he strolled home from the subway throught he heard a *whish*

2

directly overhead. There was nothing whatever blackly silhouetted against the wide stretch of moon-pale sky, yet it seemed to him that one of the moon-dimmed stars near the zenith quivered and shifted, as if there were an *eddy* in the air or sky. Heaven had wavered. And weren't there two extra stars there now?—two new stars in the center of the eddy—two dim red stars close-placed like eyes?

No, that was impossible, he must be seeing things—his own blasted fault for missing his regular soothe-session with the hypnotherapist! Just the same, he hurried his steps.

The eddy in the darkness overhead floated in pace with him a while, then swooped. He heard a louder *whish,* then something brushed his shoulder and claws seemed to fasten there for an instant.

He gasped like someone about to vomit and leaped forward frantically.

From the empty moon-glowing darkness behind him came a cackle of grim laughter.

While the householder desperately pounded upon his own front door, the eddy in the darkness shot up to the height of a sequoia, then swooped on another section of Civil Service Knolls. It hovered for a while above the imposing two-story residence of Judistrator Wisant, took a swing around the three-story one of Securitor Harker, but in the end drifted down to investigate a faintly glowing upstairs window in another three-story house.

Inside the window an athletically-handsome matron, mother of five, was leisurely preparing for bed. She was thinking, rather self-satisfiedly, that (1) she had completed all preparations for her family's participation in the Twilight Tranquility Festival tomorrow, high point of the community year; (2) she had thrown just the right amount of cold water on her eldest daughter's infatuation for the unsuitable boy visiting next door (and a hint to the hypnotherapist before her daughter's next session would do the rest); and (3) she truly didn't look five years older than her eldest daughter.

There was a tap at the window.

The matron started, pulling her robe around her, then craftily waved off the light. It had instantly occurred to her that the unsuitable boy might have had the audacity to try to visit her daughter illicitly and have mistaken bedroom windows—she had read in magazine articles that such wild lascivious young men actually existed in parts of America, though—thank Placidity!—not as regular residents of Civil Service Knolls.

She walked to the window and abruptly waved it to full transparency and then with a further series of quick side-wise waves brought the room's lights to photoflood brilliance.

At first she saw nothing but the thick foliage of the sycamore a few yards outside.

Then it seemed to her as if there were an *eddy* in the massed greenery. The leaves seemed to shift and swirl.

Then a face appeared in the eddy—a green face with the fanged grin of a devil and hotly glowing eyes that looked like twin peepholes into Hell.

The matron screamed, spun around, and sprinted into the hall, shouting the local security number toward the phone which her scream triggered into ear-straining awareness.

From beyond the window came peals of cold maniacal laughter.

Yes, fear had come to Civil Service Knolls—in fact, horror would hardly be too strong a term.

> *Some men lead perfect lives*
> *—poor devils!*
> —the notebooks of A.S.

Judistrator Wisant was awakened by a familiar insistent tingling in his left wrist. He reached out and thumbed a button. The tingling stopped. The screen beside the bed glowed into life with the handsome hatchet-face of his neighbor Securitor Harker. He touched another button, activating the tiny softspeaker and micromike relays at his ear and throat.

"Go ahead, Jack," he murmured.

Two seconds after his head had left the pillow a faint light had sprung from the walls of the room. It increased now by easy stages as he listened to a terse second-hand account of the two most startling incidents to disturb Civil Service Knolls since that tragic episode ten years ago when the kindergarten hypnotherapist went crazy and called attention to her psychosis only by the shocking posthypnotic suggestions she implanted in the toddlers' minds.

Judistrator Wisant was a large, well-built, shaven-headed man. His body, half covered now by the lapping sheet, gave the impression of controlled strength held well in reserve. His hands were big and quiet. His face was a compassionate yet disciplined mask of sanity. No one ever met him and failed to be astounded when they learned afterwards that it was his wife Beth who had been the aberrating school hypnotherapist and who was now a

5

permanent resident of the nearby mental hospital of Serenity Shoals.

The bedroom was as bare and impersonal as a gymnasium locker room. Screen, player, two short bedside shelves of which one was filled with books and tapes and neatly stacked papers, an uncurtained darkened windoor leading to a small outside balcony and now set a little ajar, the double bed itself exactly half slept in—that about completed the inventory, except for two 3-D photographs on the other bedside shelf of two smiling, tragic-eyed women who looked enough alike to be sisters of about 27 and 17. The photograph of the elder bore the inscription, "To my Husband, With all my Witchy Love. Beth," and of the younger, "To her Dear Daddikins from Gabby."

The topmost of the stacked papers was a back cover cut from a magazine demurely labeled *Individuality Unlimited*: *Monthly Bulletin*. The background was a cluster of shadowy images of weird and grim beings: vampires, werewolves, humanoid robots, witches, murderesses, "Martians," mask-wearers, naked brains with legs. A central banner shouted: *Next Month*: *Accent the Monster in You*! In the lower left-hand corner was a small sharp photo of a personable young man looking mysterious, with the legend *David Cruxon*: *Your Monster Mentor*. Clipped to the page was a things-to-do-tomorrow memo in Joel Wisant's angular script: "10 ack emma: Individuality Unlimited hearing. Warn them on injunction."

Wisant's gaze shifted more than once to this item and to the two photographs as he patiently heard out Harker's account. Finally he said, "Thanks, Jack. No, I don't think it's a prankster—what Mr. Fredericks and Mrs. Ames report seeing is no joke-shop scare-your-friends illusion. And I don't think it's anything that comes in any way from Serenity Shoals, though the overcrowding there *is* a problem and we're going to have to do something about it. What's that? No, it's nobody fooling around in an antigravity harness—they're too restricted. And we know it's nothing from *outside*—that's impossible. No, the real trouble, I'm afraid is that it's nothing at all—nothing material. Does the name Mattoon mean anything to you?

"I'm not surprised, it was a hundred years ago. But a town went mad because of an imaginary prowler, there was an epidemic of insane fear. That sort of thing happening today could be much worse. Are you familiar with Report K?

"No matter, I can give you the gist of it. You're cleared for it and ought to have it. But you *are* calling on our private line, aren't you?—this stuff is top restricted.

"Report K is simply the *true* annual statistics on mental health in America. Adjusted ones showing no significant change have been issued through the usual channels. Jack, *the real incidence of new phychoses is up* 15 *per cent in the last eight months.* Yes, it *is* pretty staggering and I *am* a close-mouthed old dog. No, it's been pretty well proved that it isn't nerve-viruses or mind-war, much as the Kremlin boys would like to see us flip and despite those irrational but persistent rumors of a Mind Bomb. Analysis is not complete, but the insanity-surge seems to be due to a variety of causes—things that we've let get out of hand and must deal with drastically."

As Wisant said those last words he was looking at the Accent-the-Monster banner on the Individuality Unlimited bulletin. His hand took a stylus, crossed out the "Warn them on" in his memo, underlined "injunction" three times and added an exclamation point.

Meanwhile he continued, "As far as Mr. Fredericks and Mrs. Ames are concerned, here's your procedure. First, instruct them to tell no one about what they thought they saw—tell them it's for the public safety—and direct them to see their hypnotherapists. Same instructions to family members and anyone to whom they may have talked. Second, find the names of their hypnotherapists, call *them* and tell them to get in touch with Dr. Andreas Snowden at Serenity Shoals—he's up on Report K and will know what reassurance-techniques or memory-wiping to advise. I depend on Snowden a lot—for that matter he's going to be with us tomorrow when we go up against Individuality Unlimited. Third, don't let anything leak to the press —that's *vital*. We must confine this outbreak of delusions before any others are infected. I don't have to tell you, Jack, that I have a reason to feel very deeply about a thing like this." (His gaze went to the photo of his wife.) "That's right, Jack, we're sanitary engineers of the mind, you and I—we hose out mental garbage!"

A rather frosty smile came into his face and stayed there while he listened again to Harker.

After a bit he said, "No, I wouldn't think of missing the Tranquility Festival—in fact they've got me leading part of it. Always proud to—and these community occasions are very important in keeping people sane. Gabby? —she's looking forward to it, too, as only a pretty, sweet-minded girl of 17 can, who's been chosen Tranquility Princess. She really makes it for me. And now hop to it, Jack, while this old man grabs himself some more shut-eye. Remember that what you're up against is delusions and hallucinations, *nothing real*."

Wisant thumbed off the phone. As his head touched

the pillow and the light in the room started to die, he nodded twice, as if to emphasize his last remark.

> *Serenity Shoals, named with a happy unintended irony, is a sizable territory in America's newest frontier; the Mountains of Madness.*
> —the notebooks of A.S.

While the scant light that filtered past the windoor died, the eddy in the darkness swung away from the house of Judistrator Wisant and sped with a kind of desperation toward the sea. The houses and lawns gave out. The wooded knolls became lower and sandier and soon gave way to a wide treeless expanse of sand holding a half dozen large institutional buildings and a tent-city besides. The buildings were mostly dark, but with stripes of dimly lit windows marking stairwells and corridors; the tent-city likewise had its dimly lit streets. Beyond them both the ghostly breakers of the Pacific were barely visible in the moonlight.

Serenity Shoals, which has been called a Sandbox for Grownups, was one of Twenty-first Century America's largest mental hospitals and now it was clearly filled beyond any planned capacity. Here dwelt the garden-variety schizos, manics, paranoids, brain-damageds, a few exotic sufferers from radiation-induced nerve sickness and spaceflight-gendered gravitational dementia and cosmic shock, and a variety of other special cases—but really all of them were simply the people who for one reason or another found it a better or at least more bearable bargain to live with their imaginings rather than even pretend to live with what society called reality.

Tonight Serenity Shoals was restless. There was more noise, more laughter and chatter and weeping, more movement of small lights along the corridors and streets, more shouts and whistles, more unscheduled night-parties and night-wanderings of patients and night-expeditions of aides, more beetle-like scurryings of sand-cars with blinking headlights, more emergencies of all sorts. It may have been the general overcrowding, or the new batch of untrained nurses and aides, or the rumor that lobotomies were being performed again, or the two new snackbars. It may even have been the moonlight—Luna disturbing the "loonies" in the best superstitious tradition.

For that matter, it may have been the eddy in the darkness that was the cause of it all.

Along the landward side of Serenity Shoals, between it and the wasteland bordering Civil Service Knolls, stretched a bright new wire fence, unpleasantly but not lethally electrified—one more evidence that Serenity Shoals was having to cope with more than its quota.

Back and forth along the line of the fence, though a hundred yards above, the eddy in the darkness beat and whirled, disturbing the starlight. There was an impression of hopeless yearning about its behavior, as if it wanted to reach its people but could not pass over the boundary.

From the mangy terrace between the permanent buildings and the nominally temporary tents, Director Andreas Snowden surveyed his schizo-manic domain. He was an elderly man with sleepy eyes and unruly white hair. He frowned, sensing an extra element in the restlessness tonight. Then his brow cleared, and smiling with tender cynicism, he recited to himself:

THE MIND SPIDER AND OTHER STORIES

> "Give me your tired, your poor,
> Your huddled masses yearning to breathe free,
> The wretched refuse of your teaming shore.
> Send these, the homeless, tempest-tost to me."

*Applies a lot more to Serenity Shoals,* he thought, *than to America these days. Though I ain't no bloody copper goddess bearing a lamp to dazzle the Dagos and I ain't got no keys to no golden doors.* (Dr. Snowden was always resolutely crude and ungrammatical in his private thoughts, perhaps in reaction to the relative gentility of his spoken utterances. He was also very sentimental.)

"Oh, hello, Doctor!" The woman darting across the corner of the terrace had stopped suddenly. It was hard to see anything about her except that she was thin.

Dr. Snowden walked toward her. "Good evening, Mrs. Wisant," he said. "Rather late for you to be up and around, isn't it?"

"I know, Doctor, but the thought-rays are very thick tonight and they sting worse than the mosquitoes. Besides I'm too excited; I couldn't sleep anyhow. My daughter is coming here tomorrow."

"Is she?" Dr. Snowden asked gently. "Odd that Joel hasn't mentioned it to me—as it happens, I'm to see your husband tomorrow on a legal matter."

"Oh, Joel doesn't know she's coming," the lady assured him. "He'd never let her if he did. He doesn't think I'm good for her ever since I started blacking out on my visits home and . . . doing things. But it isn't a plot between me and Gabby, either—*she* doesn't know she's coming."

"So? Then how are you going to manage it, Mrs. Wisant?"

"Don't try to sound so normal, Doctor!—especially when you know very well *I'm not*. I suppose *you* think that *I* think I will summon her by sending a thought-ray. Not at all. I've practically given up using thought-rays. They're not reliable and they carry yellow fever. No, Doctor, I got Gabby to come here tomorrow ten years ago."

"Now how did you do that, Mrs. Wisant? Time travel?"

"Don't be so patronizing! I merely impressed it on Gabby's mind ten years ago—after all, I *am* a trained hypnotherapist—that she should come to me when she became a princess. Now Joel writes me she's been chosen Tranquility Princess for the festival tomorrow. You see?"

"Very interesting. But don't be disappointed if—"

"Stop being a wet blanket, Doctor! Don't you have any trust in psychological techniques? I *know* she's coming. Oh the daisies, the beautiful daisies . . ."

"Then that settles it. How are they treating you here these days?"

"I have no complaints, Doctor—except I must say I don't like all these new nurses and aides. They're callow. They seem to think it's very queer of us to be crazy."

Dr. Snowden chuckled. "Some people are narrow-minded," he agreed.

"Yes, and so gullible, Doctor. Just this afternoon two of the new nurses were goggling over a magazine ad about how people should improve their personalities by becoming monsters. I ask you!"

Dr. Snowden shrugged. "I doubt whether all of us are monster material. And now perhaps you'd better . . ."

"I suppose so. Good night, Doctor."

As she was turning to go, Mrs. Wisant paused to slap her left forearm viciously.

"Thought-ray?" Dr. Snowden asked.

Mrs. Wisant looked at him sardonically. "No," she said. "Mosquito!"

> *Dull security and the dead weight of perfection breed aberration even more surely than disorder and fear.*
>
> —the notebooks of A.S.

Gabrielle Wisant, commonly called Gabby though she was anything but that, was sleeping on her back in long pink pajamas, stretched out very straight and with her arms folded across her breasts, looking more like the stone funeral effigy of a girl than a living one—an effect which the unrumpled bedclothes heightened.

The unocculted windoor let in the first cold granular light of dawn. The room was feminine, but without any special character—it seemed secretive. It had one item in common with her father's: on a low bedside stand and next to a pad of pink notepaper was another sliced-off back cover of the Individuality Unlimited bulletin. Close beside the "David Cruxon: Your Monster Mentor" photo there was a note scrawled in green ink.

> Gabs— How's this for kicks? Cruxon's Carny! or corny? Lunch with your MM same place but 130 pip emma. Big legal morning. Tell you then, Dave. (Signed and Sealed in the Monsterarium, 4 pip emma, 15 June)

The page was bowed up as if something about ten inches long were lying under it.

Gabrielle Wisant's eyes opened, though not another muscle of her moved, and they stayed that way, directed at the ceiling.

And then . . . then nothing overt happened, but it was as if the mind of Gabrielle Wisant—or the soul or spirit, call it what you will—rose from unimaginable depths to the surface of her eyes to take a long look around, like a small furtive animal that silently mounts to the mouth of its burrow to sniff the weather, ready to duck back at the slightest sudden noise or apprehension of danger— in fact, rather like the ground-hog come up to see or not to see its shadow on Candlemas Day.

With a faculty profounder than physical sight, the mind of Gabby Wisant took a long questioning look around at her world—the world of a "pretty, sweet-minded girl of 17"—to decide if it were worth living in.

Sniffing the weather of America, she became aware of a country of suntanned, slimmed-down people with smoothed-out minds, who fed contentedly on decontaminated news and ads and inspiration pieces, like hamsters on a laboratory diet. *But what were they after? What did they do for kicks? What happened to the ones whose minds wouldn't smooth, or smoothed too utterly?*

She saw the sane, civilized, secure, superior community of Civil Service Knolls, a homestead without screeching traffic or violence, without jukeboxes or juvenile delinquency, a place of sensible adults and proper children, a place so tranquil it was going to have a Tranquility Festival tonight. *But just beyond it she saw Serenity Shoals with its lost thousands living in brighter darker worlds, including one who had planted posthypnotic suggestions in children's minds like time-bombs.*

She saw a father so sane, so just, so strong, so perfectly controlled, so always right that he was not so much a man as a living statue—the statue she too tried to be every night while she slept. *And what was the statue really like under the marble? What were the heat and and color of its blood?*

She saw a witty man named David Cruxon who perhaps loved her, but who was so mixed up between his cynicism and his idealism that you might say he cancelled out. A knight without armor . . . and armor without a knight.

She saw no conventional monsters, no eddies in darkness—her mind had been hiding deep down below all night.

She saw the surface of her own mind, so sweetly smoothed by a succession of kindly hypnotherapists (and one beloved traitor who must not be named) that it was positively frightening, like a book of horrors bound in pink velvet with silk rosebuds, or the sluggish sea before a hurricane or night softly silent before a scream. She wished she had the kind of glass-bottomed boat that would let her peer below, but that was the thing above all else she must not do.

She saw herself as Tranquility Princess some twelve hours hence, receiving the muted ovation under the arching trees, candlelight twinkling back from her flared and sequinned skirt and just one leaf drifted down and caught in her fine-spun hair.

Princess . . . Princess . . . As if that word were somehow a signal, the mind of Gabby Wisant made its decision about the worth of the upper world and dove back inside, dove deep deep down. The ground-hog saw its shadow black as ink and decided to dodge the dirty weather ahead.

The *thing* that instantly took control of Gabby Wisant's body when her mind went into hiding treated that body with a savage familiarity, certainly not as if it were a statue. It sprang to its haunches in the center of the bed, snuffing the air loudly. It ripped off the pink pajamas with a complete impatience or ignorance of magnetic clasps. It switched on the lights and occulted the windoor, making it a mirror, and leered approvingly at itself and ran its hands over its torso in fierce caresses. It snatched a knife with a six-inch blade from under the bulletin cover and tried its edge on its thumb and smiled at the blood it drew and sucked it. Then it went through the inner door, utterly silent as to footsteps but breathing in loud, measured gasps like a careless tiger.

When Judistrator Wisant woke, his daughter was squatted beside him on the permanently undisturbed half of his bed, crooning to his scoutmaster's knife. She wasn't looking at him quite, or else she was looking at him sideways—he couldn't tell through the eyelash-blur of his slitted eyes.

He didn't move. He wasn't at all sure he could. He humped the back of his tongue to say "Gabby," but he knew it would come out as a croak and he wasn't even sure he could manage that. He listened to his daughter—the crooning had changed back to faintly gargling tiger-gasps—and he felt the cold sweat trickling down the sides of his face and over his naked scalp and stingingly into his eyes.

Suddenly his daughter lifted the knife high above her head, both hands locked around the hilt, and drove it down into the center of the empty, perfectly mounded pillow beside him. As it thudded home he realized with faint surprise that he hadn't moved although he'd tried to. It was as though he had contracted his muscles convulsively, but discovered that all the tendons had been cut without his knowing.

He lay there quite flaccid, watching his daughter through barely parted eyelids as she mutilated the pillow with slow savage slashes, digging in the point with a twist, and sawing off a corner. She must be sweating too—strands of her fine-spun pale gold hair clung wetly to her neck and slim shoulders. She was crooning once more, with a rippling low laugh and a soft growl for variety, and she was drooling a little. The hospital smell of the fresh-cut plastic came to him faintly.

Young male voices were singing in the distance. Judistrator Wisant's daughter seemed to hear them as soon as he did, for she stopped chopping at the pillow and held still, and then she started to sway her head and she smiled and she got off the bed with long easy movements and went to the windoor and thumbed it wide open and stood on the balcony, the knife trailing laxly from her left hand.

The singing was louder now—young male voices rather dutifully joyous in a slow marching rhythm—and now he recognized the tune. It was "America the Beautiful" but the words were different. This verse began,

> *"Oh beautiful for peaceful minds,*
> *Secure families . . ."*

17

It occurred to Wisant that it must be the youths going out at dawn to gather the boughs and deck the Great Bower, a traditional preparatory step to the Twilight Tranquility Festival. He'd have deduced it instantly if his tendons hadn't been cut . . .

But then he found that he had turned his head toward the balcony and even turned his shoulders and lifted up on one elbow a little and opened his eyes wide.

His daughter put her knife between her teeth and clambered sure-footedly onto the railing and jumped to the nearest sycamore branch and hung there swinging, like a golden-haired, long-legged, naked ape.

> *"And bring with thee*
> *Tranquility*
> *To Civil Service Knolls."*

She swung in along the branch to the trunk and laid her knife in a crotch and braced one foot there and started to swing the other and her free arm too in monkey circles.

He reached out and tried to thumb the phone button, but his hand was shaking in a four-inch arc.

He heard his daughter yell, "Yoohoo! Yoohoo, boys!"

The singing stopped.

Judistrator Wisant half scrabbled, half rolled out of bed and hurried shakingly—and he hoped noiselessly—through the door and down the hall and into his daughter's bedroom, shut the door behind him—and locked it, as he only discovered later—and grabbed her phone and punched out Securitor Harker's number.

The man he wanted answered almost immediately, a little cross with sleep.

Wisant was afraid he'd have trouble being coherent at

all. He was startled to find himself talking with practically his normal confident authority and winningness.

"Wisant, Jack. Calling from home. Emergency. I need you and your squad on the double. Yes. Pick up Dr. Sims or Armstrong on the way but don't waste time. Oh—and have your men bring ladders. Yes, and put in a quick call to Serenity Shoals for a 'copter. What? *My* authority. What? Jack, I don't want to say it now, I'm not using our private line. Well, all right, just let me think for a minute . . ."

Judistrator Wisant ordinarily never had trouble in talking his way around stark facts. And he wouldn't have had even this time, perhaps, if he hadn't just the moment before seen something that distracted him.

Then the proper twist of phrase came to him.

"Look, Jack," he said, "it's this way: Gabby has gone to join her mother. Get here *fast*."

He turned off the phone and picked up the disturbing item: the bulletin cover beside his daughter's bed. He read the note from Cruxon twice and his eyes widened and his jaw tightened.

His fear was all gone away somewhere. For the moment *all* his concerns were gone except this young man and his stupid smirking face and stupider title and his green ink.

He saw the pink pad and he picked up a dark crimson stylus and began to write rapidly in a script that was a shade larger and more angular than usual.

> *For 100 years even breakfast foods had been promoting delirious happiness and glorious peace of mind. To what end?*
>
> —the notebooks of A.S.

"Suppose you begin by backgrounding us in on what Individuality Unlimited is and how it came to be? I'm sure we all have a general idea and may know some aspects in detail, but the bold outline, from management's point of view, should be firmed. At the least it will get us talking."

This suggestion, coming from the judistrator himself, reflected the surface informality of the conference taking place in Wisant's airy chambers in central new LA. Dr. Andreas Snowden sat on the judistrator's right, doodling industriously. Securitor Harker sat on Wisant's left, while flanking the trio were two female secretaries in dark business suits similar to those men wore a century before, though of somewhat shapelier cut and lighter material.

Like all the other men in the room, Wisant was sensibly clad in singlet, business jerkin, Bermuda shorts, and sandals. A folded pink paper sticking up a little from his breast pocket provided the only faintly incongruous detail. He had been just seven minutes late to the conference, perhaps a record for fathers who have seen their daughters 'coptered off to a mental hospital two hours earlier —though only Harker knew of and so could appreciate this iron-man achievement.

A stocky man with shaggy pepper-and-salt hair and pugnacious brows stood up across the table from Wisant.

"Good idea," he said gruffly. "If we're going to be hanged, let's get the ropes around our necks. First I'd better identify us shifty-eyed miscreants. I'm Bob Diskrow, president and general manager." He then indicated the two men on his left: "Mr. Sobody, our vice president in charge of research, and Dr. Gline, IU's chief psychiatrist." He turned to the right: "Miss Rawvetch, V. P. in charge of presentation—" (A big-boned blonde flashed her eyes. She was wearing a lavender business suit with pearl buttons, wing collars and Ascot tie) "—and Mr. Cruxon, junior V.P. in charge of the . . . Monster Program." David Cruxon was identifiably the young man of the photograph with the same very dark, crewcut hair and sharply watchful eyes, but now he looked simply haggard rather than mysterious. At the momentary hesitation in Diskrow's voice he quirked a smile as rapid and almost as convulsive as a tic.

"I happen already to be acquainted with Mr. Cruxon," Wisant said with a smile, "though in no fashion prejudicial to my conducting this conference. He and my daughter know each other socially."

Diskrow stuck his hands in his pockets and rocked back on his heels reflectively.

Wisant lifted a hand. "One moment," he said. "There are some general considerations governing any judistrative conference of which I should remind us. They are in line with the general principle of government by Commission, Committee and Conference which has done so much to simplify legal problems in our times. This meeting is *private*. Press is excluded, politics are taboo. Any information you furnish about IU will be treated by us as strictly confidential and we trust you will return the courtesy regarding matters we may divulge. And this is a democratic conference. *Any* of us may speak freely.

"The suggestion has been made," Wisant continued smoothly, "that some practices of IU are against the public health and safety. After you have presented your case and made your defense—pardon my putting it that way— I may in my judicial capacity issue certain advisements. If you comply with those, the matter is settled. If you do not, the advisements immediately become injunctions and

I, in my administrative capacity, enforce them—though you may work for their removal through the regular legal channels. Understood?"

Diskrow nodded with a wry grimace. "Understood—you got us in a combined hammerlock and body scissors. (Just don't spinkle us with fire ants!) And now I'll give you that bold outline you asked for—and try to be bold about it."

He made a fist and stuck out a finger from it. "Let's get one thing straight at the start: Individuality Unlimited is no idealistic or mystical outfit with its head in orbit around the moon, and it doesn't pretend to be. We just manufacture and market a product the public is willing to fork out money for. That product is individuality." He rolled the word on his tongue.

"Over one hundred years ago people started to get seriously afraid that the Machine Age would turn them into a race of robots. That mass production and consumption, the mass media of a now instantaneous communication, the subtle and often subliminal techniques of advertising and propaganda, plus the growing use of group- and hypnotherapy would turn them into a bunch of identical puppets. That wearing the same clothes, driving the same cars, living in look-alike suburban homes, reading the same pop books and listening to the same pop programs, they'd start thinking the same thoughts and having the same feelings and urges and end up with rubber-stamp personalities.

"Make no mistake, this fear was very real," Diskrow went on, leaning his weight on the table and scowling. "It was just about the keynote of the whole Twentieth Century (and of course to some degree it's still with us). The world was getting too big for any one man to comprehend, yet people were deeply afraid of groupthink, team-life, hive-living, hypo-conformity, passive adjustment, and all the rest of it. The sociologist and analyst told them they had to play 'roles' in their family life and that didn't help much, because a role is one more rubber stamp. Other cultures like Russia offered us no hope—they seemed further along the road to robot life than we were.

"In short, people were deathly afraid of loss of identity, loss of the sense of being unique human beings. First and always they dreaded depersonalization, to give it its right name.

"Now that's where Individuality Unlimited, operating under its time-honored slogan 'Different Ways to Be Different,' got its start," Diskrow continued, making a scooping gesture, as if his right hand were IU gathering up the loose ends of existence. "At first our methods were pretty primitive or at least modest—we sold people individualized doodads to put on their cars and clothes and houses, we offered conversation kits and hobby guides, we featured Monthly Convention-Crushers and Taboo-Breakers that sounded very daring but really weren't—" (Diskrow grinned and gave a little shrug) "—and incidentally came in for a lot of ribbing on the score that we were trying to mass-produce individuality and turn out uniqueness on an assembly line. Actually a lot of our work still involves randomizing pattern-details and introducing automatic unpredictable variety into items as diverse as manufactured objects and philosophies of life.

"But in spite of the ribbing we kept going because we knew we had hold of a sound idea: that if a person can be made to *feel* he's different, if he is encouraged to take the initiative in expressing himself in even a rather trivial way, then his inner man wakes up and takes over and

23

starts to operate under his own steam. What people basically need is a periodic shot in the arm. I bunk you not when I tell you that here IU has always done and is still doing a real public service. We don't necessarily give folks new personalities, but we renew the glow of those they have. As a result they become happier workers, better citizens. We make people individuality-certain."

"Uniqueness-convinced," Miss Rawvetch put in brightly.

"Depersonalization-secure," Dr. Gline chimed. He was a small man with a large forehead and a permanent hunch to his shoulders. He added: "Only a man who is secure in his own individuality can be at one with the cosmos and really benefit from the tranquil awe-inspiring rhythms of the stars, the seasons, and the sea."

At that windy remark David Cruxon quirked a second grimace and scribbled something on the pad in front of him.

Diskrow nodded approvingly—at Gline. "Now as IU began to see the thing bigger, it had to enter new fields and accept new responsibilities. Adult education, for example—one very genuine way of making yourself more of an individual is to acquire new knowledge and skills. Three-D shows—we needed them to advertise and dramatize our techniques. Art—self-expression and a style of one's own are master keys to individuality, though they don't unlock everybody's inner doors. Philosophy—it was a big step forward for us when we were able to offer people 'A Philosophy of Life That's Yours Alone.' Religion—that too, of course, though only indirectly . . . strictly non-sectarian. Childhood lifeways—it's surprising what you can do in an individualizing way with personalized games, adult toys, imaginary companions, and secret languages—and by recapturing and adapting something of the child's vivid sense of uniqueness. Psychology—indeed yes, for a person's individuality clearly depends on how his mind is organized and how fully its resources are used. Psychiatry too—it's amazing how a knowledge of the workings of abnormal minds can be used to suggest interesting patterns for the normal mind. Why—"

Dr. Snowden cleared his throat. The noise was slight but the effect was ominous. Diskrow hurried in to say, "Of course we were well aware of the serious step we were taking in entering this field so we added to our staff a large psychology department of which Dr. Gline is the distinguished current chief."

Dr. Snowden nodded thoughtfully at his professional colleague across the table. Dr. Gline blinked and hastily nodded back. Unnoticed, David Cruxon got off a third derisive grin.

Diskrow continued: "But I do want to emphasize the psychological aspect of our work—yes, and the psychiatric program of 'Soft-Sell Your Superiority,' which last year won a Lasker Group Award of the American Public Health Association."

Miss Rawvetch broke in eagerly: "And which was dramatized to the public by that still-popular 3-D show, The Useless Five, featuring the beloved characters of the Inferior Superman, the Mediocre Mutant, the Mixed-up Martian, the Clouded Esper and Rickety Robot."

Diskrow nodded. "*And* which also has led, by our usual reverse-twist technique, to our latest program of 'Accent the Monster in You.' Might as well call it our Monster Program." He gave Wisant a frank smile. "I guess that's the item that's been bothering you gentlemen and so I'm going to let you hear about it from the young man who created it—under Dr. Gline's close supervision. Dave, it's all yours."

Dave Cruxon stood up. He wasn't as tall as one would have expected. He nodded around rapidly.

"Gentlemen," he said in a deep but stridently annoying voice, "I had a soothing little presentation worked up for you. It was designed to show that IU's Monster Program is completely trivial and one hundred percent innocuous." He let that sink in, looked around sardonically, then went on with, "Well, I'm tossing that presentation in the junk-chewer!—because I don't think it does justice to the seriousness of the situation or to the great service IU is capable of rendering the cause of public health. I may step on some toes but I'll try not to break any phalanges."

Diskrow shot him a hard look that might have started out to be warning but ended up enigmatic. Dave grinned back at his boss, then his expression became grave.

"Gentlemen," he said, "A spectre is haunting America —the spectre of Depersonalization. Mr. Diskrow and Dr. Gline mentioned it but they passed over it quickly. I won't. Because depersonalization kills the mind. It doesn't mean just a weary sense of sameness and of life getting dull, it means forgetting who you are and where you stand, it means what we laymen still persist in calling insanity."

Several pairs of eyes went sharply to him at that word. Gline's chair creaked as he turned in it. Diskrow laid a hand on the psychiatrist's sleeve as if to say, "Let him alone—maybe he's building toward a reverse angle."

"Why this very real and well-founded dread of depersonalization?" David Cruxon looked around. "I'll tell you why. It's not *primarily* the Machine Age, and it's not *primarily* because life is getting too complex to be easily grasped by any one person—though those are factors. No, it's because a lot of blinkered Americans, spoonfed a sickeningly sweet version of existence, are losing touch with the basic facts of life and death, hate and love, good and evil. In particular, due to a lot too much hypno-soothing and suggestion techniques aimed at easy tranquility, they're losing a conscious sense of the black depths in their own natures—and that's what's making them fear depersonalization *and actually making them flip*—and that's what IU's Monster-in-You Program is really designed to remedy!"

There was an eruption of comments at that, with Diskrow starting to say, "Dave doesn't mean—", Gline beginning, "I disagree. I would *not* say—", and Snowden commencing, "Now if you bring in depth psychology—" but Dave added decibels to his voice and overrode them.

"Oh yes, superficially our Monster Program just consists of hints to our customers on how to appear harmlessly and handsomely sinister, but fundamentally it's going to give people a glimpse of the real Mr. Hyde in themselves—the deviant, the cripple, the outsider, the potential rapist and torture-killer—under the sugary hypno-soothed consciousness of Dr. Jekyll. In a story or play, people always love the villain best—though they'll seldom admit it —because the villain stands for the submerged, neglected, and unloved dark half of themselves. In the Monster Program we're going to awaken that half for their own good. We're going to give some expression, for a change, to the natural love of adventure, risk, melodrama, and sheer wickedness that's part of every man!"

"Dave, you're giving an unfair picture of your own program!" Diskrow was on his feet and almost bellowing at Cruxon. "I don't know why—maybe out of some twisted sense of self-criticism or some desire for martyrdom—but you are! Gentlemen, IU is not suggesting in its new program that people become real monsters in any way—"

"Oh, aren't we?"

"Dave, shut up and sit down! You've said too much already. "I'll—"

"Gentlemen!" Wisant lifted a hand. "Let me remind you that this is a democratic conference. We can all speak freely. Any other course would be highly suspicious. So simmer down, gentlemen, simmer down." He turned toward Dave with a bland warm smile. "What Mr. Cruxon has to say interests me very much."

"I'm sure it does!" Diskrow fumed bitterly.

Dave said smoothly, "What I'm trying to get over is that people can't be pampered and soothed and wrapped away from the ugly side of reality and stay sane in the long run. Half truths kills the mind just as surely as lies. People live by the shock of reality—especially the reality of the submerged sections of their own minds. It's only when a man knows the worst about himself and other men and the world that he can really take hold of the facts—brace himself against his atoms, you might say—and achieve true tranquility. People generally don't like tragedy and horror—not with the Sunday-School side of their minds, they don't—but deep down they have to have it. They have to break down the Pollyanna Partition and find what's really on the other side. An all-sugar diet is deadly. Life can be sweet, yes, but only when the contrast of horror brings out the taste. Especially the horror in a man's heart!"

"Very interesting indeed," Dr. Snowden put in quietly, even musingly, "and most lavishly expressed, if I may say so. What Mr. Cruxon has to tell us about the dark side of the human mind—the Id, the Shadow, the Death Wish, the Sick Negative, there have been many names—is of course an elementary truth. However . . ." He paused. Diskrow, still on his feet, looked at him with suspicious incredulity, as if to say, "Whose side are *you* pretending to be on?"

The smile faded from Snowden's face. "However," he continued, "it is an equally elementary truth that it is dangerous to unlock the dark side of the mind. Not every psychotherapist—not even every analyst—" (Here his gaze flickered toward Dr. Gline) "—is really competent to handle that ticklish operation. The untrained person who attempts it can easily find himself in the position of the sorcerer's apprentice. Nevertheless . . ."

"It's like the general question of human freedom," Wisant interrupted smoothly. "Most men are simply not qualified to use all the freedoms theoretically available to them." He looked at the IU people with a questioning smile. "For example, I imagine you all know something about the antigravity harness used by a few of our special military units?—at least you know that such an item exists?"

Most of the people across the table nodded. Diskrow said, "Of course we do. We even had a demonstration model in our vaults until a few days ago." Seeing Wisant's eyebrows lift he added impressively, "IU is often asked to help introduce new devices and materials to the public. As soon as the harness was released, we were planning to have Inferior Supe use it on The Useless Five show. But then the directive came through restricting the item—largely on the grounds that it turned out to be extremely dangerous and difficult to operate—and we shipped back our model."

Wisant nodded. "Since you know that much, I can make my point about human freedom more easily. Actually (but I'll deny this if you mention it outside these chambers) the antigravity harness is not such a specialist's item. The average man can rather easily learn to operate one. In other words it is today technologically possible for us to put three billion humans in the air, flying like birds.

"But three billion humans in the air would add up to confusion, anarchy, an unimaginable aerial traffic jam. Hence—restriction and an emphasis on the dangers and extreme difficulties of using the harness. The freedom to swim through the air can't be given outright, it must be doled out gradually. The same applies to all freedoms— the freedom to love, the freedom to know the world, even the freedom to know yourself—especially your more explosive drives. Don't get me wrong now—such freedoms are fine if the person is conditioned for them." He smiled with frank pride. "That's our big job, you know: conditioning people for freedom. Using conditioning-for-freedom techniques we ended juvenile delinquency and beat the Beat Generation. We—"

"Yes, you beat them all right!" Dave breaking in again suddenly, sounded raspingly angry. "You got all the impulses such movements expressed so well battened down, so well repressed and decontaminated, that now they're coming out as aberration, deep neurosis, mania. People are conforming and adjusting so well, they're such carbon copies of each other, that now they're even all starting to flip at the same time. They were over-protected mentally and emotionally. They were shielded from the truth as if it were radio-active—and maybe in its way it is, because it can start chain reactions. They were treated

30

like halfwits and that's what we're getting. Age of Tranquility! It's the Age of Psychosis! It's an open secret that the government and its Committee for Public Sanity have been doctoring the figures on mental disease for years. They're fifty, a hundred percent greater than the published ones—no one knows how much. What's this mysterious Report K we keep hearing about? Which of us hasn't had friends and family members flipping lately? Any one can see the overcrowding at asylums, the bankruptcy of hypnotherapy. This is the year of the big payoff for generations of hysterical optimism, reassurance psychology and plain soft-soaping. It's the DTs after decades of soothing-syrup addiction!"

"That's enough, Dave!" Diskrow shouted. "You're fired! You no longer speak for IU. Get out!"

"Mr. Diskrow!" Wisant's voice was stern. "I must point out to you that you're interfering with free inquiry, not to mention individuality. What your young colleague has to say interests me more and more. Pray continue, Mr. Cruxon." He smiled like a big fat cat.

Dave answered smile with glare. "What's the use?" he said harshly. "The Monster Program's dead. You got me to cut its throat and now you'd like me to finish severing the neck, but what I did or didn't do doesn't matter a bit —you were planning to kill the Monster Program in any case. You don't want to do anything to stop the march of depersonalization. You like depersonalized people. As long as they're tranquil and manageable, you don't care—it's even okay by you if you have to keep 'em in flip-factories and put the tranquility in with a needle. Government by the three Big Cs of Commission, Committee and Conference! There's a fourth C, the biggest, and that's the one you stand for—government by Censorship! So long everybody, I hope you're happy when your wives and kids start flipping—when *you* start flipping. I'm getting out."

Wisant waited until Dave got his thumb on the door, then he called, "One moment, Mr. Cruxon!" Dave held still though he did not turn around. "Miss Sturges," Wisant continued, "would you please give this to Mr. Cruxon?" He handed her the small folded sheet of pink paper from his breast pocket. Dave shoved it in his pocket and went out.

"A purely personal matter between Mr. Cruxon and myself," Wisant explained, looking around with a smile. He swiftly reached across the table and snagged the scratchpad where Dave had been sitting. Diskrow seemed about to protest, then to think better of it.

"Very interesting," Wisant said after a moment, shaking his head. He looked up from the pad. "As you may recall, Mr. Cruxon only used his stylus once—just after Dr. Gline had said something about the awe-inspiring rhythms of the sea. Listen to what he wrote." He cleared his throat and read:

*"When the majestic ocean starts to sound like water slopping around in the bathtub, it's time to jump in."*

Wisant shook his head. "I must say I feel concerned about that young man's safety . . . his *mental* safety."

"*I* do too," Miss Rawvetch interjected, looking around with a helpless shrug. "My Lord, was there *anybody* that screwball forgot to antagonize?"

Dr. Snowden looked up quickly at Wisant. Then his gaze shifted out and he seemed to become abstracted.

Wisant continued: "Mr. Diskrow, I had best tell you now that in addition to my advisement against the Monster Program, I am going to have to issue an advisement that there be a review of the mental stability of IU's entire personnel. No personal reflection on any of you, but you can clearly see why."

Diskrow flushed but said nothing. Dr. Gline held very still. Dr. Snowden began to doodle furiously.

> *A monster is a master symbol of the secret and powerful, the dangerous and unknown, evoking the remotest mysteries of nature and human nature, the most dimly-sensed enigmas of space, time, and the hidden regions of the mind.*
> —the notebooks of A.S.

Masks of monsters brooded down from all the walls—full-lipped raven-browed Dracula, the cavern-eyed dome-foreheaded Phantom, the mighty patchwork visage of Dr. Frankenstein's charnel-man with his filmy strangely compassionate eyes, and many earlier and later fruitions of the dark half of man's imagination. Along with them were numerous stills from old horror movies (both 3-D and flat), blown-up book illustrations, monster costumes and disguises including an Ape Man's hairy hide, and several big hand-lettered slogans such as "Accent Your Monster!" "Watch out, Normality!" "America, Beware!" "Be Yourself—in Spades!" "Your Lady in Black," and "Mount to Your Monster!"

But Dave Cruxon did not look up at the walls of his "Monsterarium." Instead he smoothed out the pink note he had crumpled in his hand and read the crimson script for the dozenth time.

*Please excuse my daughter for not attending lunch today, she being detained in consequence of a massive psychosis. (Signed and Sealed on the threshold of Serenity Shoals).*

The strangest thing about Dave Cruxon's reaction to the note was that he did not notice at all simply how weird it was, how strangely the central fact was stated, how queerly the irony was expressed, how like it was to an excuse sent by a pretentious mother to her child's teacher. All he had mind for was the central fact.

Now his gaze did move to the walls. Meanwhile his hands automatically but gently smoothed the note, then opened a drawer, reached far in and took out a thick sheaf of sheets of pink notepaper with crimson script, and started to add the new note to it. As he did so a brown flattened flower slipped out of the sheaf and crawled across the back of his hand. He jerked back his hands and stood staring at the pink sheets scattered over a large black blotter and at the wholly inanimate flower.

The phone tingled his wrist. He lunged at it.

"Dave Cruxon," he identified himself hoarsely.

"Serenity Shoals, Reception. I find we do have a patient named Gabrielle Wisant. She was admitted this morning. She cannot come to the phone at present or receive visitors. I would suggest, Mr. Cruxon, that you call again in about a week or that you get in touch with—"

Dave put back the phone. His gaze went back to the walls. After a while it became fixed on one particular mask on the far wall. After another while he walked slowly over to it and reached it down. As his fingers touched it, he smiled and his shoulders relaxed, as if it reassured him.

It was the face of a devil—a green devil.

He flipped a little smooth lever that could be operated by the tongue of the wearer and the eyes glowed brilliant red. Set unobtrusively in the cheeks just below the glowing eyes were the actual eyeholes of the mask—small, but each equipped with fisheye lens so that the wearer would get a wide view.

He laid down the mask reluctantly and from a heap of costumes picked up what looked like a rather narrow silver breastplate or corselet, stiffly metallic but hinged at one side for the convenience of the person putting it on. To it were attached strong wide straps, rather like those of a parachute. A thin cable led from it to a small button-studded metal cylinder that fit in the hand. He smiled again and touched one of the buttons and the hinged breastplate rose toward the ceiling, dangling its straps and dragging upward his other hand and arm. He took his finger off the button and the breastplate sagged toward the floor. He set the whole assembly beside the mask.

Next he took up a wicked-looking pair of rather stiff gloves with horny claws set at the finger-ends. He also handled and set aside a loose one-piece suit.

What distinguished both the gloves and the coverall was that they glowed whitely even in the moderately bright light of the Monsterarium.

Finally he picked up from the piled costumes what looked at first like a large handful of nothing—or rather as if he had picked up a loose cluster of lenses and prisms made of so clear a material as to be almost invisible. In whatever direction he held it, the wall behind was distorted as if seen through a heat-shimmer or as reflected in a crazy-house mirror. Sometimes his hand holding it disappeared partly and when he thrust his other arm into it, that arm vanished.

Actually what he was holding was a robe made of a plastic textile called *light-flow fabric*. Rather like lucite, the individual threads of the light-flow fabric carried or "piped" the light entering them, but unlike lucite they spilled such light after carrying it roughly halfway around a circular course. The result was that anything draped in light-flow fabric became roughly invisible, especially against a uniform background.

Dave laid down the light-flow fabric rather more reluctantly than he had put down the mask, breastplate and other items. It was as if he had laid down a twisting shadow.

Then Dave clasped his hands behind him and began to pace. From time to time his features worked unpleasantly. The tempo of his pacing quickened. A smile came to his lips, worked into his cheeks, became a fixed, hard, graveyard grin.

Suddenly he stopped by the pile of costumes, struck an attitude, commanded hoarsely, "My hauberk, knave!" and picked up the silver breastplate and belted it around him. He tightened the straps around his thighs and shoulders, his movements now sure and swift.

Next, still grinning, he growled, "My surcoat, sirrah!" —and donned the glowing coverall.

"Vizard! Gauntlets!" He put on the green mask and the clawed gloves.

Then he took up the robe of light-flow fabric and started for the door, but he saw the scattered pink notes.

He brushed them off the black blotter, found a white stylus, and gripping it with two fingers and thumb extended from slits in the righthand gauntlet, he wrote:

*Dear Bobbie, Dr. Gee, et al,*

*By the time you read this, you will probably be hearing about me on the news channels. I'm doing one last bang-up public relations job for dear old IU. You can call it Cruxon's Crusade—the One-Man Witchcraft. I've tried out the equipment before, but only experimentally. Not this time! This time when I'm finished, no one will be able to bury the Monster Program. Wish me luck on my Big Hexperiment—you'll need it!—because the stench is going to be unendurable.*

*Your little apprentice demon, D.C.*

He threw the stylus away over his shoulder and slipped on the robe of light-flow fabric, looping part of it over his head like a cowl.

Some twenty minutes ago a depressed young man in business jerkin and shorts had entered the Monsterarium.

Now an exultant-hearted heat-shimmer, with a reserve glow under its robe of invisibility, exited from it.

*There is a batable ground between madness and sanity, though few tread it: laughter.*
                                  —the notebooks of A.S.

Andreas Snowden sat in Joel Wisant's bedroom trying to analyze his feelings of annoyance and uneasiness and dissatisfaction with himself—and also trying to decide if his duty lay here or back at Serenity Shoals.

The windoor was half open on fast-fading sunlight. Through it came a medley of hushed calls and commands, hurried footsteps, twittering female laughter, and the sounds of an amateur orchestra self-consciously tuning up—the Twilight Tranquility Festival was about to begin.

Joel Wisant sat on the edge of the bed looking toward the wall. He was dressed in green tights, jerkin, and peaked cap—a Robin Hood costume for the Festival. His face wore a grimly intent, distant expression. Snowden decided that here was a part of his reason for feeling annoyed—it is always irritating to be in the same room with someone who is communicating silently by micromike and softspeaker. He knew that Wisant was at the moment in touch with Security—not with Securitor Harker, who was downstairs and probably likewise engaged in silent phoning, but with the Central Security Station in New Angeles—but that was all he did know.

Wisant's face relaxed somewhat, though it stayed grim, and he turned quickly toward Snowden, who seized the opportunity to say, "Joel, when I came here this afternoon, I didn't know anything about—" but Wisant cut him short with:

"Hold it, Andy!—and listen to this. There have been at least a dozen new mass-hysteria outbreaks in the NLA area in the past two hours." He rapped it out tersely. "Traffic is snarled on two ground routes and swirled in three 'copter lanes. If safety devices hadn't worked perfectly there'd have been a hatful of deaths and serious injuries. There've been panics in department stores, restaurants, offices, and at least one church. The hallucinations are developing a certain amount of pattern, indicating case-to-case infection. People report something rushing invisibly through the air and buzzing them like a giant fly. I'm having the obvious lunatics held—those reporting hallucinations like green faces or devilish laughter. We can funnel 'em later to psychopathic or your place—I'll want your advice on that. The thing that bothers me most is that a garbled account of the disturbances has leaked out to the press. 'Green Demon Jolts City,' one imbecile blatted! I've given orders to have the involved 'casters and commentators picked up—got to try to limit the infection. Can you suggest any other measures I should take?"

"Why, no, Joel—it's rather out of my sphere, you know," Snowden hedged. "And I'm not too sure about your theory of infectious psychosis, though I've run across a little *folie a deux* in my time. But what I did want to talk to you about—"

"Out of your sphere, Andy? What do you mean by that?" Wisant interrupted curtly. "You're a psychologist, a psychiatrist—mass hysteria's right up your alley."

"Perhaps, but security operations aren't. And how can you be so sure, Joel, that there isn't something real behind these scares?"

"Green faces, invisible fliers, Satanic laughter?—don't be ridiculous, Andy. Why these are just the sort of outbreaks Report K predicts. They're like the two cases here last night. Wake up, man!—this is a major emergency."

"Well . . . perhaps it is. It still isn't up my alley. Get your loonies to Serenity Shoals and I'll handle them." Snowden raised his hand defensively. "Now wait a minute, Joel, there's something *I* want to say. I've had it on my mind ever since I heard about Gabby. I was shocked to hear about that, Joel—you should have told me about it earlier. Anyway, you had a big shock this morning. No, don't tell me differently—it's bound to shake a man to his roots when his daughter aberrates and does a symbolic murder on him or beside him. You simply shouldn't be

39

driving yourself the way you are. You ought to have postponed the IU hearing this morning. It could have waited."

"What?—and have taken a chance of more of that Monster material getting to the public?"

Snowden shrugged. "A day or two one way or the other could hardly have made any difference."

"I disagree," Wisant said sharply. "Even as it is, it's touched off this mass hysteria and—"

"—if it is mass hysteria—"

Wisant shook his head impatiently. "—and we had to show Cruxon up as an irresponsible mischief maker. You must admit that was a good thing."

"I suppose so," Snowden said slowly. "Though I'm rather sorry we stamped on him quite so hard—teased him into stamping on himself, really. He had hold of some very interesting ideas even if he was making bad use of them."

"How can you say that, Andy? Don't you psychologists ever take things seriously?" Wisant sounded deeply shocked. His face worked a little. "Look, Andy, I haven't told anybody this, but I think Cruxon was largely responsible for what happened to Gabby."

Snowden looked up sharply. "I keep forgetting you said they were acquainted. Joel, how deep did that go? Did they have dates? Do you think they were in love? Were they together much?"

"I don't know!" Wisant had started to pace. "Gabby didn't have dates. She wasn't old enough to be in love. She met Cruxon when he lectured to her communications class. After that she saw him in the daytime—only once or twice, I thought—to get material for her course. But there must have been things Gabby didn't tell me. I don't know how far they went, Andy, I don't know!"

He broke off because a plump woman in flowing Greek robes of green silk had darted into the room.

"Mr. Wisant, you're 'on' in ten minutes!" she cried, hopping with excitement. Then she saw Snowden. "Oh excuse me."

"That's quite all right, Mrs. Potter," Wisant told her. "I'll be there on cue."

She nodded happily, made an odd pirouette, and darted out again. Simultaneously the orchestra outside, which sounded as if composed chiefly of flutes, clarinets and recorders, began warbling mysteriously.

Snowden took the opportunity to say quickly, "Listen to me, Joel. I'm worried about the way you're driving yourself after the shock you had this morning. I thought that when you came home here you'd quit, but now I find that it's just so you can participate in this community affair while keeping in touch at the same time with those NLA scares. Easy does it, Joel—Harker and Security Central can handle those things."

Wisant looked at Snowden. "A man must attend to *all* his duties," he said simply. "This is *serious*, Andy, and any minute *you* may be involved whether you like it or not. What do you think the danger is of an outbreak at Serenity Shoals?"

"Outbreak?" Snowden said uneasily. "What do you mean?"

"I mean just that. You may think of your patients as children, Andy, but the cold fact is that you've got ten thousand dangerous maniacs not three miles from here under very inadequate guard. What if they are infected by the mass hysteria and stage an outbreak?"

Snowden frowned. "It's true we have some inadequately trained personnel these days. But you've got the wrong picture of the situation. Emotionally sick people don't stage mass outbreaks. They're not syndicate crooks with smuggled guns and dynamite."

"I'm not talking about plotted outbreaks. I'm talking about mass hysteria. If it can infect the sane, it can infect the insane. And I know the situation at Serenity Shoals has become very difficult—very difficult for you, Andy—with the overcrowding. I've been keeping in closer touch with that than you may know. I'm aware that you've petitioned that lobotomy, long-series electroshock, and heavy narcotics be reintroduced in general treatment."

"You've got that wrong," Snowden said sharply. "A minority of doctors—a couple of them with political connections—have so petitioned. I'm dead set against it myself."

"But most families have given consent for lobotomies."

"Most families don't want to be bothered with the person who goes over the edge. They're willing to settle for anything that will 'soothe' him."

"Why do you headshrinkers always have to sneer at decent family feelings?" Wisant demanded stridently. "Now you're talking like Cruxon."

"I'm talking like myself! Cruxon was right about too much soothing syrup—especially the kind you put in with a needle or a knife."

Wisant looked at him puzzledly. "I don't understand you, Andy. You'll have to do something to control your patients as the overcrowding mounts. With this epidemic mass hysteria you'll have hundreds, maybe thousands of cases in the next few weeks. Serenity Shoals will become a . . . a Mind Bomb! I always thought of you as a realist, Andy."

Snowden answered sharply, "And I think that when you talk of thousands of new cases, you're extrapolating from too little data. 'Dangerous maniacs' and 'mind bombs' are theater talk—propaganda jargon. You can't mean that, Joel."

Wisant's face was white, possibly with suppressed anger, and he was trembling very slightly. "You won't say that, Andy if your patients erupt out of Serenity Shoals and come pouring over the countryside in a great gush of madness."

Snowden stared at him. "You're afraid of them," he said softly. "That's it—you're afraid of my loonies. At the back of your mind you've got some vision of a stampede of droolers with butcher knives." Then he winced at his own words and slumped a little. "Excuse me, Joel," he said, "but really, if you think Serenity Shoals is such a dangerous place, why did you let your daughter go there?"

"Because *she* is dangerous," Wisant answered coldly. "I'm a realist, Andy."

Snowden blinked and then nodded wearily, rubbing his eyes. "I'd forgotten about this morning." He looked around. "Did it happen in this room?"

Wisant nodded.

"Where's the pillow she chopped up?" Snowden asked callously.

Wisant pointed across the room at a box that was not only wrapped and sealed as if it contained infectious material, but also corded and the cord tied in an elaborate bow. "I thought it should be carefully preserved," he said.

Snowden stared. "Did you wrap that box?"

"Yes. Why?"

Snowden said nothing.

Harker came in asking, "Been in touch with the Station the last five minutes, Joel? Two new outbreaks. A meeting of the League for Total Peace Through Total Disarmament reports that naked daggers appeared from nowhere and leaped through the air, chasing members and pinning the speaker to his rostrum by his jerkin. One man kept yelling about poltergeists—we got *him*. And the naked body of a man weighing 300 pounds fell spang in the middle of the Congress of the SPECP—that's the Society for the Prevention of Emotional Cruelty to People. Turned out to be a week-old corpse stolen from City Hospital Morgue. Very fragrant. Joel, this mass-hysteria thing is broadening out."

Wisant nodded and opened a drawer beside his bed.

Snowden snorted. "A solid corpse is about as far from mass hysteria as you can get," he observed. "What do you want with that hot-rod, Joel?"

Wisant did not answer. Harker showed surprise.

"You stuck a heat-gun in your jerkin, Joel," Snowden persisted. "Why?"

Wisant did not look at him, but waved sharply for silence. Mrs. Potter had come scampering into the room, her green robes flying.

"You're on, Mr. Wisant, you're *on*!"

He nodded at her coolly and walked toward the door just as two unhappy-looking men in business jerkins and shorts appeared in it. One of them was carrying a rolled-up black blotter.

"Mr. Wisant, we want to talk to you," Mr. Diskrow began. "I should say we *have* to talk to you. Dr. Gline

and I were making some investigations at the IU offices
—Mr. Cruxon's in particular—and we found—"

"Later," Wisant told them loudly as he strode by.

"Joel!" Harker called urgently, but Wisant did not
pause or turn his head. He went out. The four men looked
after him puzzledly.

The Twilight Tranquility Festival was approaching its
muted climax. The Pixies and Fairies (girls) had danced
their woodland ballet. The Leprechauns and Elves (boys)
had made their Flashlight Parade. The Greenest Turf,
the Growingest Garden, the Healthiest Tree, the Quietest
'Copter, the Friendliest House, the Rootedest Family, and
many other silently superlative exurban items had been
identified and duly admired. The orchestra had played all
manner of forest, brook, and bird music. The Fauns and
Pans (older boys) had sung "Tranquility So Masterful,"
"These Everlasting Knolls," the Safety Hymn, and "Come
Let's Steal Quietly." The Sprites and Nymphs (older
girls) had done their Candlelight Saraband. Representing
religion, the local Zen Buddhist pastor (an old Cauca-
sian Californian) had blessed the gathering with a sweet-
sour wordlessness. And now the everpopular Pop Wisant
was going to give his yearly talk and award trophies ("It's
tremendous of him to give of himself this way," one
matron said, "after what he went through this morning.
Did you know that she was stark naked? They wrapped
a blanket around her to put her aboard the 'copter but
she kept pulling it off.")

Freshly cut boughs attached to slim magnesium scaf-
folding made, along with the real trees, a vast leafy
bower out of what had this morning been an acre of
lawn. Proud mothers in green robes and dutiful fathers

in green jerkins lined the walls, shepherding their younger children. Before them stood a double line of Nymphs and Sprites in virginal white ballet costumes, each holding a tall white candle tipped with blue-hearted golden flame.

Up to now it had been a rather more nervously gay Tranquility Festival than most of the mothers approved. Even while the orchestra played there had been more than the usual quota of squeals, little shrieks, hysterical giggles, complaints of pinches and prods in the shadows, candles blown out, raids on the refreshment tables, small children darting into the bushes and having to be retrieved. But Pop Wisant's talk would smooth things out, the worriers told themselves.

And indeed as he strode between the ranked nymphs with an impassive smile and mounted the vine-wreathed podium, the children grew much quieter. In fact the hush that fell on the leafy Big Top was quite remarkable.

"Dear friends, charming neighbors, and fellow old coots," he began—and then noticed that most of the audience were looking up at the green ceiling.

There had been no wind that evening, no breeze at all, but some of the boughs overhead were shaking violently. Suddenly the shaking died away. ("My, what a sudden gust that was," Mrs. Ames said to her husband. Mr. Ames nodded vaguely—he had somehow been thinking of the lines from Macbeth about Birnam Wood coming to Dunsinane.)

"Fellow householders and family members of Civil Service Knolls," Wisant began again, wiping his forehead, "in a few minutes several of you will be singled out for friendly recognition, but I think the biggest award ought to go to all of you collectively for one more year of working for tranquility . . ."

The shaking of the boughs had started up again and was traveling down the far wall. At least half the eyes of the audience were traveling with it. ("George!" Mrs. Potter said to her husband, "it looks as if a lot of crumpled cellophane were being dragged through the branches. It all wiggles." He replied, "I forgot my glasses." Mr. Ames muttered to himself: "The wood began to move. Liar and slave!"

Wisant resolutely kept his eyes away from the traveling commotion and continued, ". . . and for one more year of keeping up the good fight against violence, delinquency, irrationality . . ."

A rush of wind (looking like "curdled air," some said afterwards) sped from the rear of the hall to the podium. Most of the candles were blown out, as if a giant had puffed at his giant birthday cake, and the Nymphs and Sprites squealed all the way down the double line.

The branches around Wisant shook wildly. ". . . emotionalism, supersitution, and the evil powers of the imagination!" he finished with a shout, waving his arms as if to keep off bats or bees.

Twice after that he gathered himself to continue his talk, although his audience was in a considerable uproar, but each time his attention went back to a point a little above their heads, no one else saw anything where he was looking (except some "curdled air"), but Wisant seemed to see something most horrible, for his face paled, he began to back off as if the something were approaching him, he waved out his arms wildly as one might at a wasp or a bat, and suddenly he began to scream, "Keep it off me! Can't you see it, you fools? Keep it off!"

As he stepped off the podium backwards he snatched something from inside his jerkin. There was a nasty *whish* in the air and those closest to him felt a wave of heat. There were a few shrill screams. Wisant fell heavily on the turf and did not move. A shining object skidded away from his hand. Mr. Ames picked it up. The pistol-shaped weapon was unfamiliar to him and he only later discovered it was a heat-gun.

The foliage of the Great Bower was still again, but a long streak of leaves in the ceiling had instantaneously turned brown. A few of these came floating down as if it were autumn.

> *Sometimes I think of the whole world as one great mental hospital, its finest people only inmates trying out as aides.*
>
> The notebooks of A.S.

It is more fun than skindiving to soar through the air in an antigravity harness. That is, after you have got the knack of balancing your field. It is deeply thrilling to tilt your field and swoop down at a slant, or cut it entirely and just drop—and then right it or gun it and go bounding up like a rubber ball. The positive field around your head and shoulders creates an air cushion against the buffeting of the wind and your own speed.

But after a while the harness begins to chafe, your sense of balance gets tired, your gut begins to resent the slight griping effects of the field supporting you, and the solid ground which you first viewed with contempt comes to seem more and more inviting. David Cruxon discovered all of these things.

Also, it is great fun to scare people. It is fun to flash a green demon mask in their faces out of nowhere and see them blanch. Or to glow white in the dark and listen to them scream. It is fun to snarl traffic and panic pedestrians and break up solemn gatherings—the solemner the better—with rude or shocking intrusions. It is fun to know that your fellow man is little and puffed up and easily terrified and as in love with security as a baby with his bottle, and to prove it on him again and again. Yes, it is fun to be a practicing monster.

But after a while the best of Halloween pranks becomes monotonous, fear reactions begin to seem stereotyped, you start to see yourself in your victims, and you get ashamed of winning with loaded dice. David Cruxon discovered this too.

He had thought after he broke up the Tranquility Festival that he had hours of mischief left in him. The searing near-miss of Wisant's hot-rod had left him exhilarated. (Only the light-flow fabric, diverting the infrared blast around him, had saved him from dangerous, perhaps fatal burns.) And now the idea of stampeding an insane asylum had an ironic attraction. And it *had* been good sport at first, especially when he invisibly buzzed two sand-cars of aides into a panic so that they went careening over the dunes on their fat tires, headlight beams swinging frantically, and finally burst through the light fence on the landward side (giving rise to a rumor of an erupting horde of ravening madmen). *That* had been very good fun indeed, rather like harmlessly strafing war refugees, and after it Dave had shucked off his robe and hood of invisibility and put on a Glowing Phantom aerobatic display, diving and soaring over the dark tiny hills, swooping on the little groups with menacing phosphorescent claws and peals of Satanic laughter.

But that didn't prove to be nearly as good fun. True, his victims squealed and sometimes ran, but they didn't seem to panic permanently like the aides. They seemed to stop after a few steps and come back to be scared again, like happily hysterical children. He began to wonder what must be going on in the minds down there if a Glowing Phantom were merely a welcome diversion. Then the feeling got hold of him that those people down there saw through him and sympathized with him. It was a strange feeling—both deflating and heart-warming.

But what really finished Dave off as a practicing monster was when they started to cheer him—cheer him as if he were their champion returning in triumph. Cruxon's Crusade—was that what he'd called it? And was this his Holy Land? As he asked himself that question he realized that he was drifting wearily down toward a hilltop on a long slow slant and he let his drift continue, landing with a long scuff.

Despite the cheers, he rather expected to be gibbered at and manhandled by the crowd that swiftly gathered around him. Instead he was patted on the back, congratulated for his exploits at New Angeles, and asked intelligent questions.

Gabby Wisant's mind had fully determined to stay underground a long time. But that had been on the assumptions that her body would stay near Daddikins at Civil Service Knolls and that the thing that had taken control of her body would stay hungry and eager. Now those assumptions seemed doubtful, so her mind decided to risk another look around.

She found herself one of the scattered crowd of people wandering over sandhills in the dark. Some memories came to her, even of the morning, but not painfully enough to drive her mind below. They lacked pressure.

There was an older woman beside her—a rather silly and strangely affected woman by her talk, yet somehow likable—who seemed to be trying to look after her. By stages Gabby came to realize it must be her mother.

Most of the crowd were following the movements of something that glowed whitely as it swooped and whirled through the air, like a small demented comet far off course. After a bit she saw that the comet was a phosphorescent man. She laughed.

Some of the people started to cheer. She copied them. The glowing man landed on a little sand hill just ahead. Some of the crowd hurried forward. She followed them. She saw a young man stepping clumsily out of some glowing coveralls. The glow let her see her face.

"Dave, you idiot!" she squealed at him happily.

He smiled at her shamefacedly.

Doctor Snowden found Dave and Gabby and Beth Wisant on a dune just inside the break in the wire fence—the last of the debris from last night's storm. The sky was just getting light. The old man motioned back the aides with him and trudged up the sandy rise and sat down on a log.

"Oh hello, Doctor," Beth Wisant said. "Have you met Gabrielle? She came to visit me just like I told you."

Dr. Snowden nodded tiredly. "Welcome to Serenity Shoals, Miss Wisant. Glad to have you here."

Gabby smiled at him timidly. "I'm glad to be here too —I think. Yesterday . . ." Her voice trailed off.

"Yesterday you were a wild animal," Beth Wisant said loudly, "and you killed a pillow instead of your father. The doctor will tell you that's very good sense."

Dr. Snowden said, "All of us have these somatic wild animals—" (He looked at Dave) "—these monsters."

Gabby said, "Doctor, do you think that Mama calling me so long ago can have had anything to do with what happened to me yesterday?"

"I see no reason why not," he replied, nodding. "Of course there's a lot more than that that's mixed up about you."

"When *I* implant a suggestion, it works," Beth Wisant asserted.

Gabby frowned. "Part of the mix-up is in the world, not me."

"The world is always mixed up," Dr. Snowden said. "It's a pretty crazy hodge-podge with sensible strains running through it, if you look for them very closely. That's one of the things we have to accept." He rubbed his eyes and looked up. "And while we're on the general topic of unpleasant facts, here's something else. Serenity Shoals has got itself one more new patient besides yourselves—Joel Wisant."

"Hum," said Beth Wisant. "Maybe now that I don't have him to go home to, I can start getting better."

"Poor Daddikins," Gabby said dully.

"Yes," Snowden continued, looking at Dave, "that last little show you put on at the Tranquility Festival—and then on top of it the news that there was an outbreak here—really broke him up." He shook his head. "Iron perfectionist. At the end he was even demanding that we drop an atomic bomb on Serenity Shoals—that was what swung Harker around to my side."

"An atom bomb!" Beth Wisant said. "The idea!"

Dr. Snowden nodded. "It does seem a little extreme."

"So you class me as a psychotic too," Dave said, a shade argumentively. "Of course I'll admit that after what I did—"

Dr. Snowden looked at him sourly. "*I* don't class you as psychotic at all—though a lot of my last-century colleagues would have taken great delight in tagging you as a psychopathic personality. I think you're just a spoiled and willful young man with no capacity to bear frustration. You're a self-dramatizer. You jumped into the ocean of aberration—that was the meaning of your note, wasn't it?—but the first waves tossed you back on the beach. Still, you got in here, which was your main object."

"How do you know that?" Dave asked.

"You'd be surprised," Dr. Snowden said wearily, "at how many more-or-less sane people want to get into mental hospitals these days—it's probably the main truth behind the Report K figures. They seem to think that insanity is the only great adventure left man in a rather depersonalizing age. They want to understand their fellow man at the depths, and here at least they get the opportunity." He looked at Dave meaningfully as he said that. Then he went on, "At any rate, Serenity Shoals is the safest place for you right now, Mr. Cruxon. It gets you out from under a stack of damage suits and maybe a lynch-mob or two."

He stood up. "So come on then, all of you, down to Receiving," he directed, a bit grumpily. "Pick up that junk you've got there, Dave, and bring it along. We'll try to hang onto the harness—it might be useful in treating gravitational dementia. Come on, come on!—I've wasted all night on you. Don't expect such concessions in the future. Serenity Shoals is no vacation resort—and no honeymoon resort either!—though . . ." (He smiled flickeringly) ". . . though some couples do try."

They followed him down the sandy hill. The rising sun

behind them struck gold from the drab buildings and faded tents ahead.

Dr. Snowden dropped back beside Dave. "Tell me one thing," he said quietly. "Was it fun being a green demon?"

Dave said, "That it was!"

# DAMNATION MORNING

Time traveling, which is not quite the good clean boyish fun it's cracked up to be, started for me when this woman with the sigil on her forehead looked in on me from the open doorway of the hotel bedroom where I'd hidden myself and the bottles and asked me, "Look, Buster, do you want to live?"

It was the sort of question that would have suited a religious crackpot of the strong-arm, save-your-soul variety, but she didn't look like one. And I might very well have answered it—in fact I almost did—with a hangover, one percent humorous, "Good God, no!" Or—a poor second —I could have studied the dark, dust-burnished arabesques of the faded blue carpet for a perversely long time and then countered with a grudging, "Oh, if you insist."

But I didn't, perhaps because there didn't seem to be anything like one percent of humor in the situation. Point One: I have been blacked out the past half hour or so—this woman might just have opened the door or she might have been watching me for ten minutes. Point Two: I was in the fringes of DTs, trying to come off a big drunk. Point Three: I knew for certain that I had just killed someone or left him or her to die, though I hadn't the faintest idea of whom or why.

Let me try to picture my state of mind a little more vividly. My consciousness, the sentient self-aware part of me, was a single quivering point in the center of an endless plane vibrating harshly with misery and menace. I was like a man in a rowboat in the middle of the Pacific —or better, I was like a man in a shellhole in the North African desert (I served under Montgomery and any region adjoining the DTs is certainly a No Man's Land). Around me, in every direction—this is my consciousness I'm describing, remember—miles of flat burning sand, nothing more. Way beyond the horizon were two divorced wives, some estranged children, assorted jobs, and other unexceptional wreckage. Much closer, but still beyond the horizon, were State Hospital (twice) and Psycho (four times). Shallowly buried very near at hand, or perhaps blackening in the open just behind me in the shellhole, was the person I had killed.

But remember that I knew I had killed a real person. *That* wasn't anything allegorical.

Now for a little more detail on this "Look, Buster," woman. To begin with, she didn't resemble any part of the DTs or its outlying kingdoms, though an amateur might have thought differently—especially if he had given too much weight to the sigil on her forehead. But I was no amateur.

She seemed about my age—forty-five—but I couldn't be sure. Her body looked younger than that, her face older; both were trim and had seen a lot of use, I got the impression. She was wearing black sandals and a black unbelted tunic with just a hint of the sack dress to it, yet she seemed dressed for the street. It occurred to me even then (off-track ideas can come to you very swiftly and sharply in the DT outskirts) that it was a costume that, except perhaps for the color, would have fitted into any number of historical eras: old Egypt, Greece, maybe the Directoire, World War I, Burma, Yucatan, to name some. (Should I ask her if she spoke Mayathan? I didn't, but I don't think the question would have fazed her; she seemed altogether sophisticated, a real cosmopolite—she pronounced "Buster" as if it were part of a curious, somewhat ridiculous jargon she was using for shock purposes.)

From her left arm hung a black handbag that closed with a drawstring and from which protruded the tip of silvery object about which I found myself apprehensively curious.

Her right arm was raised and bent, the elbow touching the door frame, the hand brushing back the very dark bangs from her forehead to show me the sigil, as if that had a bearing on her question.

The sigil was an eight-limbed asterisk made of fine dark lines and about as big as a silver dollar. An X superimposed on a plus sign. It looked permanent.

Except for the bangs she wore her hair pinned up. Her ears were flat, thin-edged, and nicely shaped, with the long lobes that in Chinese art mark the philosopher. Small square silver flats with rounded corners ornamented them.

Her face might have been painted by Toulouse-Lautrec or Degas. The skin was webbed with very fine lines; the eyes were darkly shadowed and there was a touch of green on the lids (Egyptian?—I asked myself); her mouth was wide, tolerant, but realistic. Yes, beyond all else, she seemed realistic.

And as I've indicated, I was ready for realism, so when she asked, "Do you want to live?" I somehow managed not to let slip any of the flippant answers that came flocking into my mouth, I realized that this was the one time in a million when a big question is really meant and your answer really counts and there are no second chances, I realized that the line of my life had come to one of those points where there's a kink in it and the wrong (or maybe the right) tug can break it and that as far as I was concerned at the present moment, she knew all about everything.

So I thought for a bit, not long, and I answered, "Yes."

She nodded—not as if she approved my decision, or disapproved it for that matter, but merely as if she accepted it as a basis for negotiations—and she let her bangs fall back across her forehead. Then she gave me a quick dry smile and she said, "In that case you and I have got to get out of here and do some talking."

For me that smile was the first break in the shell—the shell around my rancid consciousness or perhaps the dark, star-pricked shell around the space-time continuum.

"Come on," she said. "No, just as you are. Don't stop for anything and—" (She caught the direction of my immediate natural movement) "—*don't look behind you* if you meant that about wanting to live."

Ordinarily being told not to look behind you is a remarkably silly piece of advice, it makes you think of those "pursuing fiend" horror stories that scare children, and you look around automatically—if only to prove you're no child. Also in this present case there was my very real and dreadful curiosity: I wanted terribly (yes, terribly) to know whom it was I had just killed—a forgotten third wife? a stray woman? a jealous husband or boyfriend? (though I seemed too cracked up for love affairs) the hotel clerk? a fellow derelict?

But somehow, as with her "want to live" question, I had the sense to realize that this was one of those times when the usually silly statement is dead serious, that she meant her warning quite literally.

If I looked behind me, I would die.

I looked straight ahead as I stepped past the scattered brown empty bottles and the thin fume mounting from the tiny crater in the carpet where I'd dropped a live cigarette.

As I followed her through the door I caught, from the window behind me, the distant note of a police siren.

Before we reached the elevator the siren was nearer and it sounded as if the fire department had been called out too.

I saw a silvery flicker ahead. There was a big mirror facing the elevators.

"What I told you about not looking behind you goes for mirrors too," my conductress informed me. "Until I tell you differently."

The instant she said that, I knew that I had forgotten what I looked like; I simply could not visualize that dreadful witness (generally inhabiting a smeary bathroom mirror) of so many foggy mornings: my own face. One glance in the mirror . . .

But I told myself: realism. I saw a blur of brown shoes and black sandals in the big mirror, nothing more.

The cage of the right-hand elevator, dark and empty, was stopped at this floor. A crosswise wooden bar held the door open. My conductress removed the bar and we stepped inside. The door closed and she touched the controls. I wondered, "Which way will it go? Sideways?"

It began to sink normally. I started to touch my face, but didn't. I started to try to remember my name, but stopped. It would be bad tactics, I thought, to let myself become aware of any more gaps in my knowledge. I knew I was alive. I would stick with that for a while.

The cage sank two and a half floors and stopped, its doorway blocked by the drab purple wall of the shaft. My conductress switched on the tiny dome light and turned to me.

"Well?" she said.

I put my last thought into words.

"I'm alive," I said, "and I'm in your hands."

She laughed lightly. "You find it a compromising situation? But you're quite correct. You accepted life from me, or through me, rather. Does that suggest anything to you?"

My memory may have been lousy, but another, long unused section of my mind was clicking. "When you get anything," I said, "you have to pay for it and sometimes money isn't enough, though I've only once or twice been in situations where money didn't help."

"Three times now," she said. "Here is how it stacks up: You've bought your way with something other than money, into an organization of which I am an agent. Or perhaps you'd rather go back to the room where I recruited you? We might just be able to manage it."

Through the walls of the cage and shaft I could hear the sirens going full blast, underlining her words.

I shook my head. I said, "I think I knew that—I mean, that I was joining an organization—when I answered your first question."

"It's a very big organization," she went on, as if warning me. "Call it an empire or a power if you like. So far as you are concerned, it has always existed and always will exist. It has agents everywhere, literally. Space and time are no barriers to it. Its purpose, so far as you will ever be able to know it, is to change, for its own aggrandizement, not only the present and future, but also the past. It is a ruthlessly competitive organization and is merciless to its employees."

"I. G. Farben?" I asked grabbing nervously and clumsily at humor.

She didn't rebuke my flippancy, but said, "And it isn't the Communist Party or the Ku Klux Klan, or the Avenging Angels or the Black Hand, either, though its enemies give it a nastier name."

"Which is?" I asked.

"The Spiders," she said.

That word gave me the shudders, coming so suddenly. I expected the sigil to step off her forehead and scuttle down her face and leap at me—something like that.

She watched me. "You might call it the Double Cross," she suggested, "if that seems better."

"Well, at least you don't try to prettify your organization," was all I could think to say.

She shook her head. "With the really big ones you don't have to. You never know if the side into which you are born or reborn is 'right' or 'good'—you only know that it's your side and you try to learn about it and form an opinion as you live and serve."

"You talk about sides," I said. "Is there another?"

"We won't go into that now," she said, "but if you ever meet someone with an S on his forehead, he's not a friend, no matter what else he may be to you. *That* S stands for Snakes."

I don't know why *that* word coming just then, gave me so much worse a scare—crystallized all my fears, as it were—but it did. Maybe it was only some little thing, like Snakes meaning DTs. Whatever it was, I felt myself turning to mush.

"Maybe we'd better go back to the room where you found me," I heard myself saying. I don't think I meant it, though I surely felt it. The sirens had stopped, but I could hear a lot of general hubbub, outside the hotel and inside it too, I thought—noise from the other elevator shaft and it seemed to me, from the floor we'd just left— hurrying footsteps, taut voices, something being dragged. I knew terror here, in this stalled elevator, but the *loudness* outside would be worse.

"It's too late now," my conductress informed me. She slitted her eyes at me. "You see, Buster," she said, *"You're still back in that room.* You might be able to handle the problem of rejoining yourself if you went back alone, but not with other people around."

"What did you do to me?" I said very softly.

"I'm a Resurrectionist," she said as quietly. "I dig bodies out of the space-time continuum and give them the freedom of the fourth dimension. When I Resurrected you, I cut you out of your lifeline close to the point that you think of as the Now."

"My lifeline?" I interrupted. "Something in my palm?"

"All of you from your birth to your death," she said. "A you-shaped rope embedded in the space-time con- tinuum—I cut you out of it. Or I made a fork in your lifeline, if you want to think of it that way, and you're in the free branch. But the other you, the buried you, the one people think of as the real you, is back in your room with the other Zombies going through the motions."

"But how can you cut people out of their lifelines?"

I asked. "As a bull-session theory, perhaps. But to actually do it—"

"You can if you have the proper tool," she said flatly swinging her handbag. "Any number of agents might have done it. A Snake might have done it as easily as a Spider. Might still—but we won't go into that."

"But if you've cut me out of my lifeline," I said, "and given me the freedom of the fourth dimension, why are we in the same old space—time? That is, if this elevator still is?"

"It is," she assured me. "We're still in the same space-time because I haven't led us out of it. We're moving through it at the same temporal speed as the you we left behind, keeping pace with his Now. But we both have an added mode of freedom, at present imperceptible and inoperative. Don't worry, I'll make a Door and get us out of here soon enough—if you pass the test."

I stopped trying to understand her metaphysics. Maybe I was between floors with a maniac. Maybe I was a maniac myself. No matter—I would just go on clinging to what felt like reality. "Look," I said, "that person I murdered, or left to die, is he back in the room too? Did you see him—or her?"

She looked at me and then nodded. She said carefully, "The person you killed or doomed is still in the room."

An aching impulse twisted me a little. "Maybe I should try to go back—" I began. "Try to go back and unite the selves . . ."

"It's too late now," she repeated.

"But I want to," I persisted. "There's something pulling at me, like a chain hooked to my chest."

She smiled unpleasantly. "Of course there is," she said.

"It's the vampire in you—the same thing that drew me to your room or would draw any Spider or Snake. The blood scent of the person you killed or doomed."

I drew back from her. "Why do you keep saying 'or'?" I blustered. "I didn't look but you must have *seen*. You must *know*. *Whom did I kill?* And what is the Zombie me doing back there in that room with the body?"

"There's no time for that now," she said, spreading the mouth of her handbag. "Later you can go back and find out, if you pass the test."

She drew from her handbag a pale gray gleaming implement that looked by quick turns to me like a knife, a gun, a slim scepter, and a delicate branding iron— especially when its tip sprouted an eight-limbed star of silver wire.

"The test?" I faltered, staring at the thing.

"Yes, to determine whether you can live in the fourth dimension or only die in it."

The star began to spin, slowly at first, then faster and faster. Then it held still, but something that was part of it or created by it went on spinning like a Helmholtz color wheel—a fugitive, flashing rainbow spiral. It looked like the brain's own circular scanning pattern become visible and that frightened me because that is what you see at the onset of alcoholic hallucinations.

"Close your eyes," she said.

I wanted to jerk away, I wanted to lunge at her, but I didn't dare. Something might shake loose in my brain if I did. The spiral flashed through the wiry fringe of my eyebrows as she moved it closer. I closed my eyes.

Something stung my forehead icily, like ether, and I instantly felt that I was moving forward with an easy

64

rise and fall, as if I were riding a very gentle roller-coaster. There was a low pulsing roar in my ears.

I snapped my eyes open. The illusion vanished. I was standing stock still in the elevator and the only sounds were the continuing hubbub that had succeeded the sirens. My conductress was smiling at me, encouragingly.

I closed my eyes again. Instantly I was surging forward through the dark on the gentle roller-coaster and the hubbub was an almost musical roar that rose and fell. Smoky lights showed ahead. I glided through a cobble-stoned alleyway where cloaked and broad-hatted bravoes with rapiers swinging at their sides turned their heads to stare at me knowingly, while women in gaudy dresses that swept the dirt leered in a way that was half inviting, half contemptuous.

Darkness swallowed them. An iron gate clanged behind me. Bluer, cleaner lights sprang up. I passed a field studded with tall silver ships. Tall, slender-limbed men and women in blue and silver smocks broke off their tasks or games to watch me—evenly but a little sadly, I thought. They drifted out of sight behind me and another gate clanged. For a moment the pulsing sound shaped itself into words: "There's a road to travel. It's a road that's wide . . ."

I opened my eyes again. I was back in the stalled elevator, hearing the muted hubbub, facing my smiling conductress. It was very strange—an illusion that could be turned on or off by lowering or raising the eyelids. I remembered fleetingly that the brain's alpha rhythm, which may be the rhythm of its scanning pattern idling, vanishes when you open your eyes and I wondered if the roller-coaster was the alpha rhythm.

When I closed my eyes this time I plunged deeper into the illusion. I burst through many scenes: a street of flashing swords, the central aisle of a dark cavernous factory filled with unknown untended machines, a Chinese pavilion, a Harlem nightclub, a square filled with brightly-painted statues and noisy white-togaed men, a humped road across which a ragged muddy-footed throng fled in terror from a porticoed temple which showed only as wide bars of light rising in a mist from behind a low hill.

And always the half-music pulsed without cease. From time to time I heard the "Road to Travel" song repeated with two endings, now one, now another: "It leads around the cosmos to the other side," and "It leads to insanity or suicide."

I could have whichever ending I chose, it seemed to me—I needed only to will it.

And then it burst on me that I could go wherever I wanted, see whatever I wanted, just by willing it. I was traveling along that dark mysterious avenue, swaying and undulating in every dimension of freedom, that leads to every hidden vista of the unconscious mind, to any and every spot in space and time—the avenue of the adventurer freed from all limitations.

I grudgingly opened my eyes again to the stalled elevator. "This is the test?" I asked my conductress quickly. She nodded, watching me speculatively, no longer smiling. I dove eagerly back into the darkness.

In the exultation of my newly realized power I skimmed a universe of sensation, darting like a bird or bee from scene to scene: a battle, a banquet, a pyramid a-building, a tatter-sailed ship in a storm, beasts of all descriptions a torture chamber, a death ward, a dance, an orgy, a leprosary, a satellite launching, a stop at a dead star between galaxies, a newly-created android rising from a silver vat, a witch-burning, a cave birth, a crucifixion . . .

Suddenly I was afraid. I had gone so far, seen so much, so many gates had clanged behind me, and there was no sign of my free flight stopping or even slowing down. I could control where I went but not whether I went—I had to keep on going. And going. And going.

My mind was tired. When your mind is tired and you want to sleep you close your eyes. But if, whenever you close your eyes, you start going again, you start traveling the road . . .

I opened mine. "How do I ever sleep?" I asked the woman. My voice had gone hoarse.

She didn't answer. Her expression told me nothing. Suddenly I was very frightened. But at the same time I was horribly tired, mind and body, I closed my eyes . . .

I was standing on a narrow ledge that gritted under the soles of my shoes whenever I inched a step one way or another to ease the cramps in my leg muscles. My hands and the back of my head were flattened against a gritty wall. Sweat stung my eyes and trickled inside my collar. There was a medley of voices I was trying not to hear. Voices far below.

I looked down at the toes of my shoes, which jutted out a little over the edge of the ledge. The brown leather was dusty and dull. I studied each gash in it, each rolled or loose peeling of tanned surface, each pale shallow pit.

Around the toes of my shoes a crowd of people clustered, but small, very small—tiny oval faces mounted crosswise on oval bodies that were scarcely larger—navy beans each mounted on a kidney bean. Among them were red and black rectangles, proportionately small—police cars and fire trucks. Between the toes of my shoes was an empty gray space.

In spirit or actuality, I was back in the body I had left in the hotel bedroom, the body that had climbed through the window and was threatening to jump.

I could see from the corner of my eye that someone in black was standing beside me, in spirit or actuality. I tried to turn my head and see who it was, but that instant the invisible roller-coaster seized me and I surged forward and—this time down.

The faces started to swell. Slowly.

A great scream puffed up at me from them. I tried to ride it but it wouldn't hold me. I plunged on down, face first.

The faces below continued to swell. Faster. Much faster, and then . . .

One of them looked *all matted hair* except for the forehead, which had an S on it.

My fall took me past that horror face and then checked three feet from the gray pavement (I could see fine, dust-drifted cracks and a trodden wad of chewing gun) and without pause I shot upward again, like a high diver who fetches bottom, or as if I'd hit an invisible sponge-rubber cushion yards thick.

I soared upward in a great curve, losing speed all the time, and landed without a jar on the ledge from which I'd just fallen.

Beside me stood the woman in black. A gust of wind ruffled her bangs and I saw the eight-limbed sigil on her forehead.

I felt a surge of desire and I put my arms around her and pulled her face toward mine.

She smiled but she dipped her head so that our foreheads touched instead of our lips.

Ether ice shocked my brain. I closed my eyes for an instant.

When I opened them we were back in the stalled elevator and she was drawing away from me with a smile and I felt a wonderful strength and freshness and power, as if all avenues were open to me now without compulsion, as if all space and time were my private preserve.

I closed my eyes and there was only blackness quiet as the grave and close as a caress. No roller-coaster, no scanning pattern digging movement and faces from the dark, no realms of the DT fringes. I laughed and I opened my eyes.

My conductress was at the controls of the elevator and we were dropping smoothly and her smile was sardonic but comradely now, as if we were fellow professionals.

The elevator stopped and the door slid open on the crowded lobby and we stepped out arm in arm. My partner checked a moment in her stride and I saw her lift an "Out of Order" sign off the door and drop it behind the sand vase.

We strode toward the entrance. I knew what Zombies were now—the people around me, hotel folk, public, cops, firemen. They were all staring toward the entrance, where the revolving doors were pinned open, as if they were waiting (an eternity, if necessary) for something to happen. They didn't see us at all—except that one or two trembled uneasily, like folk touched by nightmares, as we brushed past them.

As we went through the doorway my partner said to me rapidly, "When we get outside do whatever you have to, but when I touch your shoulder come with me. There'll be a Door behind you."

Once more she drew the gray implement from her handbag and there was a silver spinning beside me. I did not look at it.

I walked out into empty sidewalk and a scream that came from dozens of throats. Hot sunlight struck my face. We were the only souls for ten yards around, then came a line of policemen and the screaming mob. Everyone of them was looking straight up, except for a man in dirty shirtsleeves who was pushing his way, head down, between two cops.

You know the sound when a butcher slams a chunk of beef down on the chopping block? I heard that now, only much bigger. I blinked my eyes and there was a body on its back in the middle of the empty space and the finest spray of blood was misting down on the gray sidewalk.

I sprang forward and knelt beside the body, vaguely aware that the man who had pushed between the cops was doing the same from the other side. I studied the face of the man who had leaped to his death.

The face was unmarred, though it was rather closer to the sidewalk than it would have been if the back of the head had been intact. It was a face with a week's beard on it that rose higher than the cheekbones—the big forehead was the only sizable space on it clear of hair. It was the tormented face of a drunk, but now at peace. It was a face I knew, in fact had always known. It was simply the face my conductress had not let me see, the face of the person I had doomed to die: myself.

I lifted my hand and this time I let it touch the week's

growth of beard matting my face. Well, I thought, I had given the crowd an exciting half hour.

I lifted my eyes and there on the other side of the body was the dirty-sleeved man. It was the same beard-matted face as that on the ground between us, the same beard-matted face as my own.

On the forehead was a black S that looked permanent.

He was staring at my face—and then at my forehead—with a surprise, and then a horror, that I knew my own features were registering too as I stared at him. A hand touched my shoulder.

My conductress had told me that you never know whether the side into which you are born or reborn is "right" or "good." Now, as I turned and saw the shimmering silver man-high Door behind me, and her hand vanishing into it, and as I stepped through, past a rim of velvet blackness and stars, I clung to that memory, for I knew that I would be fighting on both sides forever.

# THE OLDEST SOLDIER

The one we called the Lieutnant took a long swallow of his dark Lowensbrau. He'd just been describing a battle of infantry rockets on the Eastern Front, the German and Russian positions erupting bundles of flame.

Max swished his paler beer in its green bottle and his eyes got a faraway look and he said, "When the rockets killed their thousands in Copenhagen, they laced the sky with fire and lit up the steeples in the city and the masts and bare spars of the British ships like a field of crosses."

"I didn't know there were any landings in Denmark," someone remarked with an expectant casualness.

"This was in the Napoleonic wars," Max explained. "The British bombarded the city and captured the Danish fleet. Back in 1807."

"Vas you dere, Maxie?" Woody asked, and the gang around the counter chuckled and beamed. Drinking at a liquor store is a pretty dull occupation and one is grateful for small vaudeville acts.

"Why bare spars?" someone asked.

"So there'd be less chance of the rockets setting the launching ships afire," Max came back at him. "Sails burn fast and wooden ships are tinder anyway—that's why ships firing red-hot shot never worked out. Rockets and bare spars were bad enough. Yes, and it was Congreve rockets made the 'red glare' at Fort McHenry," he continued unruffled, "while the 'bombs bursting in air' were about the earliest precision artillery shells, fired from mortars on bomb-ketches. There's a condensed history of arms in the American anthem." He looked around smiling.

"Yes, I was there, Woody—just as I was with the South Martians when they stormed Copernicus in the Second Colonial War. And just as I'll be in a foxhole outside Copeybawa a billion years from now while the blast waves from the battling Venusian spaceships shake the soil and roil the mud and give me some more digging to do."

This time the gang really snorted its happy laughter and Woody was slowly shaking his head and repeating, "Copenhagen and Copernicus and—what was the third? Oh, what a mind he's got," and the Lieutnant was saying, "Yah, you vas there—in books," and I was thinking, *Thank God for all the screwballs, especially the brave ones who never flinch, who never lose their tempers or drop the act, so that you never do quite find out whether it's just a gag or their solemnest belief. There's only one person here takes Max even one percent seriously, but they all love him because he won't ever drop his guard. . . .*

"The only point I was trying to make," Max continued when he could easily make himself heard "was the way styles in weapons keep moving in cycles."

"Did the Romans use rockets?" asked the same light voice as had remarked about the landings in Denmark and the bare spars. I saw now it was Sol from behind the counter.

Max shook his head. "Not so you'd notice. Catapults were their specialty." He squinted his eyes. "Though now you mention it, I recall a dogfoot telling me Archimedes faked up some rockets powdered with Greek fire to touch off the sails of the Roman ships at Syracuse—and none of this romance about a giant burning glass."

"You mean," said Woody, "that there are other gaze-bos besides yourself in this fighting-all-over-the-universe-and-to-the-end-of-time racket?" His deep whiskey voice was at its solemnest and most wondering.

"Naturally," Max told him earnestly. "How else do you suppose wars ever get really fought and refought?"

"Why should wars ever be refought?" Sol asked lightly. "Once ought to be enough."

"Do you suppose anybody could time-travel and keep his hands off wars?" Max countered.

I put in my two cents' worth. "Then that would make Archimedes' rockets the earliest liquid-fuel rockets by a long shot."

Max looked straight at me, a special quirk in his smile. "Yes, I guess so," he said after a couple of seconds. "On this planet, that is."

The laughter had been falling off, but that brought it back and while Woody was saying loudly to himself, "I like that refighting part—that's what we're all so good at," the Lieutnant asked Max with only a moderate accent that fit North Chicago, "And zo you aggshually have fought on Mars?"

"Yes, I have," Max agreed after a bit. "Though that ruckus I mentioned happened on our moon—expeditionary forces from the Red Planet."

"Ach, yes. And now let me ask you something—"

I really mean that about screwballs, you know. I don't care whether they're saucer addicts or extrasensory perception bugs or religious or musical maniacs or crackpot philosophers or pychologists or merely guys with a strange dream or gag like Max—for my money they are the ones who are keeping individuality alive in this age of conformity. They are the ones who are resisting the encroachments of the mass media and motivation research and the mass man. The only really bad thing about crack pottery and screwballistics (as with dope and prostitution) is the coldblooded people who prey on it for money. So I say to all screwballs: Go it on your own. Don't take any wooden nickels or give out any silver dimes. Be wise and brave—like Max.

He and the Lieutnant were working up a discussion of the problems of artillery in airless space and low gravity that was a little too technical to keep the laughter alive. So Woody up and remarked, "Say, Maximillian, if you got to be in all these wars all over hell and gone, you must have a pretty tight schedule. How come you got time to be drinking with us bums?"

"I often ask myself that," Max cracked back at him. "Fact is, I'm on a sort of unscheduled furlough, result of a transportation slip-up. I'm due to be picked up and returned to my outfit any day now—that is, if the enemy underground doesn't get to me first."

It was just then, as Max said that bit about enemy underground, and as the laughter came, a little diminished, and as Woody was chortling "Enemy underground now. How do you like that?" and as I was thinking how much Max had given me in these couple of weeks —a guy with an almost poetic flare for vivid historical

75

reconstruction, but with more than that . . . it was just then that I saw the two red eyes low down in the dusty plate-glass window looking in from the dark street.

Everything in modern America has to have a big plate glass display window, everything from suburban mansions, general managers' offices and skyscraper apartments to barber shops and beauty parlors and ginmills —there are even gymnasium swimming pools with plate glass windows twenty feet high opening on busy boulevards—and Sol's dingy liquor store was no exception; in fact I believe there's a law that it's got to be that way. But I was the only one of the gang who happened to be looking out of this particular window at the moment. It was a dark windy night outside and it's a dark untidy street at best and across from Sol's are more plate glass windows that sometimes give off very odd reflections, so when I got a glimpse of this black formless head with the two eyes like red coals peering in past the brown pyramid of empty whiskey bottles, I don't suppose it was a half second before I realized it must be something like a couple of cigarette butts kept alive by the wind, or more likely a freak reflection of tail lights from some car turning a corner down street, and in another half second it was gone, the car having finished turning the corner or the wind blowing the cigarette butts away altogether. Still, for a moment it gave me a very goosey feeling, coming right on top of that remark about an enemy underground.

And I must have shown my reaction in some way, for Woody, who is very observant, called out, "Hey, Fred, has that soda pop you drink started to rot your nerves— or are even Max's friends getting sick at the outrageous lies he's been telling us?"

76

Max looked at me sharply and perhaps he saw something too. At any rate he finished his beer and said, "I guess I'll be taking off." He didn't say it to me particularly, but he kept looking at me. I nodded and put down on the counter my small green bottle, still one-third full of the lemon pop I find overly sweet, though it was the sourest Sol stocked. Max and I zipped up our windbreakers. He opened the door and a little of the wind came in and troubled the tanbark around the sill. The Lieutnant said to Max, "Tomorrow night we design a better space gun;" Sol routinely advised the two of us, "Keep your noses clean;" and Woody called, "So long space soldiers." (And I could imagine him saying as the door closed, "That Max is nuttier than a fruitcake and Freddy isn't much better. Drinking soda pop—ugh!")

And then Max and I were outside leaning into the wind, our eyes slitted against the blown dust, for the three-block trudge to Max's pad—a name his tiny apartment merits without any attempt to force the language.

There weren't any large black shaggy dogs with red eyes slinking about and I hadn't quite expected there would be.

Why Max and his soldier-of-history gag and our outwardly small comradeship meant so much to me is something that goes way back into my childhood. I was a lonely timid child, with no brothers and sisters to spar around with in preparation for the battles of life, and I never went through the usual stages of boyhood gangs either. In line with those things I grew up into a very devout liberal and "hated war" with a mystical fervor during the intermission between 1918 and 1939—so much so that I made a point of avoiding military services in the second conflict, though merely by working in the nearest war plant, not by the arduously heroic route of out-and-out pacifism.

But then the inevitable reaction set in, sparked by the liberal curse of being able, however, belatedly, to see both sides of any question. I began to be curious about and cautiously admiring of soldiering and soldiers. Unwillingly at first, I came to see the necessity and romance of the spearmen—those guardians, often lonely as myself, of the perilous camps of civilization and brotherhood in a black hostile universe . . . necessary guardians, for all the truth in the indictments that war caters to irrationality and sadism and serves the munition makers and reaction.

I commenced to see my own hatred of war as in part only a mask for cowardice, and I started to look for some way to do honor in my life to the other half of the truth. Though it's anything but easy to give yourself a feeling of being brave just because you suddenly want that feeling. Obvious opportunities to be obviously brave come very seldom in our largely civilized culture, in fact they're clean contrary to safety drives and so-called normal adjustment and good peacetime citizenship and all the rest, and they come mostly in the earliest part of a man's life. So that for the person who belatedly wants to be brave it's generally a matter of waiting for an opportunity for six months and then getting a tiny one and muffing it in six seconds.

But however uncomfortable it was, I had this reaction to my devout early pacifism, as I say. At first I took it out only in reading. I devoured war books, current and historical, fact and fiction. I tried to soak up the military aspects and jargon of all ages, the organization and weapons, the strategy and tactics. Characters like Tros of

Samothrace and Horatio Hornblower became my new secret heroes, along with Heinlein's space cadets and Bullard and other brave rangers of the spaceways.

But after a while reading wasn't enough. I had to have some real soldiers and I finally found them in the little gang that gathered nightly at Sol's liquor store. It's funny but liquor stores that serve drinks have a clientele with more character and comradeship than the clienteles of most bars—perhaps it is the absence of juke-boxes, chromium plate, bowling machines, trouble-hunting, drink-cadging women, and—along with those—men in search of fights and forgetfulness. At any rate, it was at Sol's liquor store that I found Woody and the Lieutnant and Bert and Mike and Pierre and Sol himself. The casual customer would hardly have guessed that they were anything but quiet souses, certainly not soldiers, but I got a clue or two and I started to hang around, making myself inconspicuous and drinking my rather symbolic soda pop, and pretty soon they started to open up and yarn about North Africa and Stalingrad and Anzio and Korea and such and I was pretty happy in a partial sort of way.

And then about a month ago Max had turned up and he was the man I'd really been looking for. A genuine soldier with my historical slant on things—only he knew a lot more than I did, I was a rank amateur by comparison—and he had this crazy appealing gag too, and besides that he actually cottoned to me and invited me on to his place a few times, so that with him I was more than a tavern hanger-on. Max was good for me, though I still hadn't the faintest idea of who he really was or what he did.

Naturally Max hadn't opened up the first couple of nights with the gang, he'd just bought his beer and kept quiet and felt his way much as I had. Yet he looked and felt so much the soldier that I think the gang was inclined to accept him from the start—a quick stocky man with big hands and a leathery face and smiling tired eyes that seemed to have seen everything at one time or another. And then on the third or fourth night Bert told something about the Battle of the Bulge and Max chimed in with some things he'd seen there, and I could tell from the looks Bert and the Lieutnant exchanged that Max had "passed"—he was now the accepted seventh member of the gang, with me still as the tolerated clerical-type hanger-on, for I'd never made any secret of my complete lack of military experience.

Not long afterwards—it couldn't have been more than one or two nights—Woody told some tall tales and Max started matching him and that was the beginning of the time-and-space-soldier gag. It was funny about the gag. I suppose we just should have assumed that Max was a history nut and liked to parade his bookish hobby in a picturesque way—and maybe some of the gang did assume just that—but he was so vivid yet so casual in his descriptions of other times and places that you felt there had to be something more and sometimes he'd get such a lost, nostalgic look on his face talking of things fifty million miles or five hundred years away that Woody would almost die laughing, which was really the sincerest sort of tribute to Max's convincingness.

Max even kept up the gag when he and I were alone together, walking or at his place—he'd never come to mine—though he kept it up in a minor-key sort of way, so that it sometimes seemed that what he was trying to get across was not that he was the Soldier of a Power that was fighting across all of time to change history, but simply that we men were creatures with imaginations and it was our highest duty to try to feel what it was really like to live in other times and places and bodies. Once he said to me, "The growth of consciousness is everything, Fred—the seed of awareness sending its roots across space and time. But it can grow in so many ways, spinning its web from mind to mind like the spider or burrowing into the unconscious darkness like the snake. The biggest wars are the wars of thought."

But whatever he was trying to get across, I went along with his gag—which seems to me the proper way to behave with any other man, screwball or not, so long as you can do it without violating your own personality. Another man brings a little life and excitement into the world, why try to kill it? It is simply a matter of politeness and style.

I'd come to think a lot about style since knowing Max. It doesn't matter so much what you do in life, he once said to me—soldiering or clerking, preaching or picking pockets—so long as you do it with style. Better fail in a grand style than succeed in a mean one—you won't enjoy the successes you get the second way.

Max seemed to understand my own special problems without my having to confess them. He pointed out to me that the soldier is trained for bravery. The whole object of military discipline is to make sure that when the six seconds of testing come every six months or so, you do the brave thing without thinking, by drilled second nature. It's not a matter of the soldier having some special virtue or virility the civilian lacks. And then about fear. All men are afraid, Max said, except a few psychopathic or suicidal types and they merely haven't fear at the conscious level. But the better you know yourself and the men around you and the situation you're up against (though you can never know all of the last and sometimes you have only a glimmering), then the better you are prepared to prevent fear from mastering you. Generally speaking, if you prepare yourself by the daily self-discipline of looking squarely at life, if you imagine realistically the troubles and opportunities that may come, then the chances are you won't fail in the testing. Well, of course I'd heard and read all those things before, but coming from Max they seemed to mean a lot more to me. As I say, Max was good for me.

So on this night when Max had talked about Copenhagen and Copernicus and Copeybawa and I'd imagined I'd seen a big black dog with red eyes and we were walking the lonely streets hunched in our jackets and I was listening to the big clock over at the University tolling eleven . . . well, on this night I wasn't thinking anything special except that I was with my screwball buddy and pretty soon we'd be at his place and having a nightcap. I'd make mine coffee.

I certainly wasn't expecting anything.

Until, at the windy corner just before his place, Max suddenly stopped.

Max's junky front room-and-a-half was in a smoky brick building two fights up over some run-down stores. There is a rust-flaked fire escape on the front of it, running past the old-fashioned jutting bay windows, its lowest flight a counterbalanced one that only swings down when somebody walks out onto it—that is, if a person ever had occasion to.

When Max stopped suddenly, I stopped too of course. He was looking up at his window. His window was dark and I couldn't see anything in particular, except that he or somebody else had apparently left a big black bundle of something out on the fire-escape and—it wouldn't be the first time I'd seen that space used for storage and drying wash and what not, against all fire regulations, I'm sure.

But Max stayed stopped and kept on looking.

"Say, Fred," he said softly then, "how about going over to your place for a change? Is the standing invitation still out?"

"Sure Max, why not," I replied instantly, matching my voice to his. "I've been asking you all along."

My place was just two blocks away. We'd only have to turn the corner we were standing on and we'd be headed straight for it.

"Okay then," Max said. "Let's get going." There was a touch of sharp impatience in his voice that I'd never heard there before. He suddenly seemed very eager that we should get around that corner. He took hold of my arm.

He was no longer looking up at the fire escape, but I was. The wind had abruptly died and it was very still. As we went around the corner—to be exact as Max pulled me around it—the big bundle of something lifted up and looked down at me with eyes like two red coals.

I didn't let out a gasp or say anything. I don't think Max realized then that I'd seen anything, but I was shaken. This time I couldn't lay it to cigarette butts or reflected tail lights, they were too difficult to place on a third-story fire escape. This time my mind would have to rationalize a lot more inventively to find an explanation, and until it did I would have to believe that something . . . well, alien . . . was at large in this part of Chicago.

Big cities have their natural menaces—hold-up artists,

hopped-up kids, sick-headed sadists, that sort of thing—and you're more or less prepared for them. You're not prepared for something . . . alien. If you hear a scuttling in the basement you assume it's rats and although you know rats can be dangerous you're not particularly frightened and you may even go down to investigate. You don't expect to find bird-catching Amazonian spiders.

The wind hadn't resumed yet. We'd gone about a third of the way down the first block when I heard behind us, faintly but distinctly, a rusty creaking ending in a metallic jar that didn't fit anything but the first flight of the fire escape swinging down to the sidewalk.

I just kept walking then, but my mind split in two—half of it listening and straining back over my shoulder, the other half darting off to investigate the weirdest notions, such as that Max was a refugee from some unimaginable concentration camp on the other side of the stars. If there were such concentration camps, I told myself in my cold hysteria, run by some sort of supernatural SS men, they'd have dogs just like the one I'd thought I'd seen . . . and, to be honest, thought I'd *see* padding along if I looked over my shoulder now.

It was hard to hang on and just walk, not run, with this insanity or whatever it was hovering over my mind, and the fact that Max didn't say a word didn't help either.

Finally, as we were starting the second block, I got hold of myself and I quietly reported to Max exactly what I thought I'd seen. His response surprised me.

"What's the layout of your apartment, Fred? Third floor, isn't it?"

"Yes. Well . . ."

"Begin at the door we'll be going in," he directed me. "That's the living room, then there's a tiny short open hall, then the kitchen. It's like an hour-glass, with the living room and kitchen the ends, and the hall the wasp waist. Two doors open from the hall: the one to your right (figuring from the living room) opens into the bathroom; the one to your left, into a small bedroom."

"Windows?"

"Two in the living room, side by side," I told him. "None in the bathroom. One in the bedroom, onto an air shaft. Two in the kitchen, apart."

"Back door in the kitchen?" he asked.

"Yes. To the back porch. Has glass in the top half of it. I hadn't thought about that. That makes three windows in the kitchen."

"Are the shades in the windows pulled down now?"

"No."

Questions and answers had been rapid-fire, without time for me to think, done while we walked a quarter of a block. Now after the briefest pause Max said, "Look, Fred, I'm not asking you or anyone to believe in all the things's I've been telling as if for kicks at Sol's—that's too much for all of a sudden—but you do believe in that black dog, don't you?" He touched my arm warningly. "No, don't look behind you!"

I swallowed. "I believe in him right now," I said.

"Okay. Keep on walking. I'm sorry I got you into this, Fred, but now I've got to try to get both of us out. *Your* best chance is to disregard the thing, pretend you're not aware of anything strange happening—then the beast won't know whether I've told you anything, it'll be hesitant to disturb you, it'll try to get at me without troubling you, and it'll even hold off a while if it thinks it will get me that way. But it won't hold off forever—it's only imperfectly disciplined. *My* best chance is to get in touch with headquarters—something I've been putting off—and have them pull me out. I should be able to do it in an hour, maybe less. You can give me that time, Fred."

"How?" I asked him. I was mounting the steps to the vestibule. I thought I could hear, very faintly, a light pad-padding behind us. I didn't look back.

Max stepped through the door I held open and we started up the stairs.

"As soon as we get in your apartment," he said, "you turn on all the lights in the living room and kitchen. Leave the shades up. Then start doing whatever you might be doing if you were staying up at this time of night. Reading or typing, say. Or having a bite of food, if you can manage it. Play it as naturally as you can. If you hear things, if you feel things, try to take no notice. Above all, don't open the windows or doors, or look out of them to see anything, or go to them if you can help it —you'll probably feel drawn to do just that. Just play it naturally. If you can hold them . . . it . . . off that way for half an hour or so—until midnight, say—if you can give me that much time, I should be able to handle my end of it. And remember, it's the best chance for you as well as for me. Once I'm out of here, you're safe."

"But you—" I said, digging for my key, "—what will you—?"

"As soon as we get inside," Max said, "I'll duck in your bedroom and shut the door. Pay no attention. Don't come after me, whatever you hear. Is there a plug-in in your bedroom? I'll need juice."

"Yes," I told him, turning the key. "But the lights have been going off a lot lately. Someone has been blowing the fuses."

"That's great," he growled, following me inside.

I turned on the lights and went in the kitchen, did the same there and came back. Max was still in the living room, bent over the table beside my typewriter. He had a sheet of light-green paper. He must have brought it with him. He was scrawling something at the top and bottom of it. He straightened up and gave it to me.

"Fold it up and put it in your pocket and keep it on you the next few days," he said.

It was just a blank sheet of cracklingly thin light-green paper with "Dear Fred" scribbled at the top and "Your friend, Max Bournemann" at the bottom and nothing in between.

"But what—?" I began, looking up at him.

"Do as I say!" He snapped at me. Then, as I almost flinched away from him, he grinned—a great big comradely grin.

"Okay, let's get working," he said, and he went into the bedroom and shut the door behind him.

I folded the sheet of paper three times and unzipped my wind-breaker and tucked it inside the breast pocket. Then I went to the bookcase and pulled at random a volume out of the top shelf—my psychology shelf, I remembered the next moment—and sat down and opened the book and looked at a page without seeing the print.

And now there was time for me to think. Since I'd spoken of the red eyes to Max there had been no time for anything but to listen and to remember and to act. Now there was time for me to think.

My first thoughts were: *This is ridiculous! I saw something strange and frightening, sure, but it was in the dark, I couldn't see anything clearly, there must be some simple natural explanation for whatever it was on the fire escape. I saw something strange and Max sensed I was frightened and when I told him about it he decided to play a practical joke on me in line with that eternal gag he lives by. I'll bet right now he's lying on my bed and chuckling, wondering how long it'll be before I—*

The window beside me rattled as if the wind had suddenly risen again. The rattling grew more violent—and then it abruptly stopped without dying away, stopped with a feeling of tension, as if the wind or something more material were still pressing against the pane.

And I did not turn my head to look at it, although (or perhaps because) I knew there was no fire escape or other support outside. I simply endured that sense of a presence at my elbow and stared unseeingly at the book in my hands, while my heart pounded and my skin froze and flushed.

I realized fully then that my first skeptical thoughts had been the sheerest automatic escapism and that, just as I'd told Max, I believed with my whole mind in the black dog. I believed in the whole business insofar as I could imagine it. I believed that there are undreamed of powers warring in this universe. I believed that Max was a stranded time-traveller and that in my bedroom he was now frantically operating some unearthly device to signal for help from some unknown headquarters. I believed that the impossible and the deadly was loose in Chicago.

But my thoughts couldn't carry further than that. They kept repeating themselves, faster and faster. My mind felt like an engine that is shaking itself to pieces. And the impulse to turn my head and look out the window came to me and grew.

I forced myself to focus on the middle of the page where I had the book open and start reading.

*Jung's archetype transgress the barriers of time and space. More than that: they are capable of breaking the shackles of the laws of causality. They are endowed with frankly mystical "prospective" faculties. The soul itself, according to Jung, is the reaction of the personality to the unconscious and includes in every person both male and female elements, the animus and anima, as well as the persona or the person's reaction to the outside world. . . .*

I think I read the last sentence a dozen times, swiftly at first, then word by word, until it was a meaningless jumble and I could no longer force my gaze across it.

Then the glass in the window beside me creaked.

I laid down the book and stood up, eyes front, and went into the kitchen and grabbed a handful of crackers and opened the refrigerator.

The rattling that muted itself in hungry pressure followed. I heard it first in one kitchen window, then the other, then in the glass in the top of the door. I didn't look.

I went back in the living room, hesitated a moment beside my typewriter, which had a blank sheet of yellow paper in it, then sat down again in the armchair beside the window, putting the crackers and the half carton of milk on the little table beside me. I picked up the book I'd tried to read and put it on my knees.

The rattling returned with me—at once and peremptorily, as if something were growing impatient.

I couldn't focus on the print any more. I picked up a cracker and put it down. I touched the cold milk carton and my throat constricted and I drew my fingers away.

I looked at my typewriter and then I thought of the blank sheet of *green* paper and the explanation for Max's strange act suddenly seemed clear to me. Whatever happened to him tonight, he wanted me to be able to type a message over his signature that would exonerate me. A suicide note, say. Whatever happened to him . . .

The window beside me shook violently, as if at a terrific gust.

It occurred to me that while I must not look out of the window as if expecting to see something (that would be the sort of give-away against which Max warned me) I could safely let my gaze slide across it—say, if I turned to look at the clock behind me. Only, I told myself, I mustn't pause or react if I saw anything.

I nerved myself. After all, I told myself, there was the blessed possibility that I would see nothing outside the taut pane but darkness.

I turned my head to look at the clock.

I saw *it* twice, going and coming back, and although my gaze did not pause or falter, my blood and my thoughts started to pound as if my heart and mind would burst.

*It* was about two feet outside the window—a face or mask or muzzle of a more gleaming black than the darkness around it. The face was at the same time the face of a hound, a panther, a giant bat, and a man—in between those four. A pitiless, hopeless man-animal face alive with knowledge but dead with a monstrous melancholy and a monstrous malice. There was the sheen of needlelike white teeth against black lips or dewlaps. There was the dull pulsing glow of eyes like red coals.

My gaze didn't pause or falter or go back—yes—and my heart and mind didn't burst, but I stood up then and stepped jerkily to the typewriter and sat down at it and started to pound the keys. After a while my gaze stopped blurring and I started to see what I was typing. The first thing I'd typed was:

> the quick red fox jumped over the crazy black dog . . .

I kept on typing. It was better than reading. Typing I was doing something, I could discharge. I typed a flood of fragments: "Now is the time for all good men—", the first words of the Declaration of Independence and the Constitution, the Winston commercial, six lines of Hamlet's "To be or not to be," without punctuation, Newton's Third Law of Motion, "Mary had a big black—"

In the middle of it all the face of the electric clock that I'd looked at sprang into my mind. My mental image of it had been blanked out until then. The hands were at a quarter of twelve.

Whipping in a fresh yellow sheet, I typed the first stanza of Poe's "Ravin," the Oath of Allegiance to the American Flag, the lost-ghost lines from Thomas Wolfe, The Creed and the Lord's prayer, "Beauty is truth; truth, blackness—"

The rattling made a swift circuit of the windows—though I heard nothing from the bedroom, nothing at all—and finally the rattling settled on the kitchen door. There was a creaking of wood and metal under pressure.

I thought: *You are standing guard. You are standing guard for yourself and for Max.* And then the second thought came: *If you open the door, if you welcome it in, if you open the kitchen door and then the bedroom door, it will spare you, it will not hurt you.*

Over and over again I fought down that second thought

and the urge that went with it. It didn't seem to be coming from my mind, but from the outside. I typed Ford, Buick, the names of all the automobiles I could remember, Overland Moon, I typed all the four-letter words, I typed the alphabet, lower case and capitals, I typed the numerals and punctuation marks, I typed the keys of the keyboard in order from left to right, top to bottom, then in from each side alternately. I filled the last yellow sheet I was on and it fell out and I kept pounding mechanically, making shiny black marks on the dull black platen.

But then the urge became something I could not resist. I stood up and in the sudden silence I walked through the hall to the back door, looking down at the floor and resisting, dragging each step as much as I could.

My hands touched the knob and the long-handled key in the lock. My body pressed the door, which seemed to surge against me, so that I felt it was only my counterpressure that kept it from bursting open in a shower of splintered glass and wood.

Far off, as if it were something happening in another universe, I heard the University clock tolling One . . . two . . .

And then, because I could resist no longer, I turned the key and the knob.

The lights all went out.

In the darkness the door pushed open against me and something came in past me like a gust of cold black wind with streaks of heat in it.

I heard the bedroom door swing open.

The clock completed its strokes. Eleven . . . twelve . . .

Nothing . . . nothing at all. All pressures lifted from me. I was aware only of being alone, utterly alone. I knew it, deep down.

After some . . . minutes, I think, I shut and locked the door and I went over and opened a drawer and rummaged out a candle, lit it, and went through the apartment and into the bedroom.

Max wasn't there. I'd known he wouldn't be. I didn't know how badly I'd failed him. I lay down on the bed and after a while I began to sob and, after another while, I slept.

Next day I told the janitor about the lights. He gave me a funny look.

"I know," he said. "I just put in a new fuse this morning. I never saw one blown like that before. The window in the fuse was gone and there was a metal sprayed all over the inside of the box."

That afternoon I got Max's message. I'd gone for a walk in the park and was sitting on a bench beside the lagoon, watching the water ripple in the breeze when I felt something burning against my chest. For a moment I thought I'd dropped my cigarette butt inside my windbreaker. I reached in and touched something hot in my pocket and jerked it out. It was the sheet of green paper Max had given me. Tiny threads of smoke were rising from it.

I flipped it open and read, in a scrawl that smoked and grew blacker instant by instant:

*Thought you'd like to know I got through okay. Just in time. I'm back with my outfit. It's not too bad. Thanks for the rearguard action.*

The handwriting (thought-writing?) of the blackening

scrawl was identical with the salutation above and the signature below.

And then the sheet burst into flame. I flipped it away from me. Two boys launching a model sailboat looked at the paper flaming, blackening, whitening, disintegrating . . .

I know enough chemistry to know that paper smeared with wet white phosphorus will burst into flame when it dries completely. And I know there are kinds of invisible writing that are brought out by heat. There are those general sorts of possibility. Chemical writing.

And then there's thoughtwriting, which is nothing but a word I've coined. Writing from a distance—a literal telegram.

And there may be a combination of the two—chemical writing activated by thought from a distance . . . from a great distance.

I don't know. I simply don't know. When I remember that last night with Max, there are parts of it I doubt. But there's one part I never doubt.

When the gang asks me, "Where's Max?" I just shrug.

But when they get to talking about withdrawals they've covered; rearguard actions they've been in, I remember mine. I've never told them about it, but I never doubt that it took place.

# MIDNIGHT IN THE
# MIRROR WORLD

As the clock downstairs began to clang out midnight's twelve strokes, Giles Nefandor glanced into one of the two big mirrors between which he was passing on his nightly trip, regular as clockwork, from the telescopes on the roof to the pianos and chessboards in the living room.

What he saw there made him stop and blink and stare.

He was two steps above the mid-stair landing, where the great wrought-iron chandelier with its freight of live and dead electric bulbs swung in the chill fierce gusts of wind coming through the broken, lead-webbed, diamond-paned windows. It swung like a pendulum—a wilder yet more ponderous pendulum than that in the tall clock twanging relentlessly downstairs. He stayed aware of its menace as he peered in the mirror.

Since there was a second mirror behind him, what he saw in the one he faced was not a single reflection of himself, but many, each smaller and dimmer than the one in front of it—a half-spread stack of reflections going off toward infinity. Each reflection, except the eighth, showed against a background of mirror-gloom only his dark lean aquiline face, or at least the edge of it—from bucket-size down to dime-size—peering back at him intently from under its sleek crown of black, silver-shot hair.

But in the eighth reflection his hair was wildly disordered and his face was leaden-green, gape-jawed, and bulging-eyed with horror.

Also, his eighth reflection was not alone. Beside it was a thin black figure from which a ribbony black arm reached out and lay on his reflected shoulder. He could see only the edge of the black figure—most of it was hidden by the reflected gilt mirror frame—but he was sure it was thin.

The look of horror on his face in that reflection was so intense and so suggestive of strangulation that he clutched at his throat with both hands.

All his reflections, from the nearly life-size giants to the Lilliputians, copied this sudden gesture—except the eighth.

The eleventh stroke of midnight resounded brassily. An especially fierce gust of wind blew the chandelier closer to him so that one of its black hook-fingered arms approached his shoulder and he cringed away from it before he recognized it for the familiar object it was. It should have been hung higher, he was such a tall man, and he should have had the window repaired, but his head missed the chandelier except when the wind blew hard and after he'd been unable to find a craftsman who could work leaded glass, he had not bothered about either chore.

The twelfth stroke clanged.

When he looked into the mirror the next instant, all strangeness was gone. His eighth reflection was like the rest. All his reflections were alike, even the dimmest most distant ones that melted into mirror smoke. And there was no sign of a black figure in any one of them, although he peered until his vision blurred.

He continued downstairs, choosing a moment when the

chandelier was swinging away from him. He went immediately to his Steinway and played Scriabin preludes and sonatas until dawn, fighting the wind with them until it slunk away, then analyzed chess positions in the latest Russian tournament until the oppressive daylight had wearied him enough for sleep. From time to time he thought about what he had glimpsed in the mirror, and each time it seemed to him more likely that the disordered eighth reflection had been an optical illusion. His eyes had been strained and weary with star-gazing when it had happened. There had been those rushing shadows from the swinging chandelier, or even his narrow black necktie blown by the wind, while the thin black figure might have been simply a partial second reflection of his own black clothes—imperfections in the mirror could explain why these things had stood out only in the eighth reflection. For that matter the odd appearance of his face in that reflection might have been due to no more than a tarnished spot in the mirror's silvering. Like this whole vast house—and himself—the mirror was decaying.

He awoke when the first stars, winking on in the sky of deepening blue, signaled his personal dawn. He had almost forgotten the incident of the mirror by the time he went upstairs, donned stadium boots and hooded long sheepskin coat in the cupola room, and went out on the widow's walk to uncap his telescopes and take up his star-gazing. He made, as he realized, a quite medieval figure, except that the intruders in his heavens were not comets mostly, but Earth satellites moving at their characteristic crawl of twenty-some minutes from zenith to horizon.

He resolved a difficult double in Canis Major and was almost certain he saw a pale gas front advancing across the blackness of the Horsehead Nebula.

Finally he capped and shrouded his instruments and went inside. Habit started him downstairs and put him between the mirrors above the landing at the same minute and second of the day as he had arrived at that spot last night. There was no wind and the black chandelier with its asymmatric constellation of bulbs hung motionless on its black chain. No reeling shadows tonight. Otherwise everything was exactly the same.

And while the clock struck twelve, he saw in the mirror exactly what he had seen last night: tiny pale horror-struck Nefandor-face, black ribbon-arm touching its shoulder or neck, as if arresting him or summoning him to some doom. Tonight perhaps a little more of the black figure showed, as if it peered with one indistinguishable eye around the tinied gold frame.

Only this time it was not the eighth reflection that showed these abnormalities, but the seventh.

And this time when the glassy aberration vanished with the twelfth brassy stroke, he found it less easy to keep his thoughts from dwelling obsessively on the event. He also found himself groping for an explanation in terms of an hallucination rather than an optical illusion: an optical illusion that came so pat two nights running was hardly credible. And yet an hallucination that confined itself to only one in a stack of reflections was also most odd.

Most of all, the elusive malignity of the thin black figure struck him much more forcibly than it had the previous night. An hallucination—or ghost or demon—that met you face to face was one thing. You could strike out at it, hysterically claw at it, try to drive your fist through it. But a black ghost that lurked in a mirror, and not only that but in the deepest depths of a mirror, behind many panes of thick glass (somehow the reflected panes seemed as real as the actual ones), working its evil will on your powerless shrunken image there—that implied a craftiness and caution and horrid calculation which fitted very well with the figure's cat-and-mousing advance from the eighth reflection to the seventh. The implication was that here was a being who hated Giles Nefandor with demonic intensity.

This night and morning he avoided the eerie Scriabin and played only dancingly brisk pieces by Mozart, while the chess games he analyzed were frolicsome attacking ones by Anderssen, Kieseritzky, and the youthful Steinitz.

He had decided to wait another twenty-four hours and then if the figure appeared a third time, systematically analyze the matter and decide on what steps to take.

Yet meanwhile he could not wholly keep himself from searching his memory for people whom he had injured to the degree that they would bear him a bitter and enduring hatred. But although he searched quite conscientiously, by snatches, through the five and a half decades over which his memory stretched, he found no very likely candidates for the position of Arch-Hater or Hater to the Death of Giles Nefandor. He was a gentle person and, cushioned by inherited wealth, had never had to commit a murder or steal a large sum of money. He had wived, begat, divorced—or rather, been divorced. His wife had remarried profitably, his children were successful in far places, he had enough money to maintain his long body and his tall house while both moldered and to indulge his mild passions for the most ethereal of the arts, the most coolly aloof of the sciences, and the most darkly profound of the games.

Professional rivals? He no longer played in chess tournaments, confining his activities in that direction to a few correspondence games. He gave no more piano recitals. While his contributions to astronomical journals were of the fewest and involved no disputes.

Women? At the time of his divorce, he had hoped it would free him to find new relationships, but his lonely habits had proved too comfortable and strong and he had never taken up the search. Perhaps in his vanity he had dreaded failure—or merely the effort.

At this point he became aware of a memory buried in his mind, like a dark seed, but it refused to come clear. Something about chess? . . . no . . .

Really, he had done nothing much to anyone, for good or ill, he decided. Why should anyone hate him for doing nothing?—hate him enough to chase his image through mirrors?—he asked himself fruitlessly as he watched Kieseritzky's black queen implacably pursue Anderssen's white king.

The next night he carefully timed his descent of the stairs, using his precision clocks in the cupola—with the result that (precision machinery proving less reliable than habit) the downstairs clock had already struck five strokes when he thrust himself breathlessly between the mirrors above the landing. But his greenish horrorstruck face was there—in the sixth reflection this time, as he'd fatalistically assumed it would be—and the slender black figure was there too with outstretched arm; this time he seemed to detect that it was wearing a veil or stocking-mask: he could distinguish none of its features, but there was a faint shimmering in the face area, rather like the pale gas front he had once again detected crossing the Horsehead Nebula.

This night he completely altered his routine, neither opening a piano nor setting out any of the chessmen. Instead he lay for an hour with eyes shut, to rest them, and then spent the rest of the night and morning investigating reflections of reflections in the mirrors on the stairs and in two somewhat smaller ones which he set up in the living room and tilted by the fractional inch to get the best effects.

By the end of that time he had made a number of interesting discoveries. He'd noted reflections of reflections before, especially on the stairs, and been amused by their oddity, but he'd never thought about them systematically and certainly never experimented with them. They turned out to be a fascinating little field of study—vest-pocket optics—a science in miniature.

Vest-pocket wasn't such a bad designation, because you had to stick your vest and yourself between the two mirrors in order to observe the phenomena. Though come to think of it, you ought to be able to do the same thing with a periscope held sideways, by that means introducing your vision between the mirrors without introducing yourself. It might be worth trying.

But getting back to basics, when you stood between nearly parallel mirrors, looking at one, you saw first the direct reflection of your face, next the reflection of the back of your head in the mirror behind you; then, barely visible around those two, you saw the second reflection of your face, really just an edge of hair and cheek and ear; then the second reflection of the back of your head, and so on. As the heads grew smaller, you saw more of each, until the entire face became visible, quite tiny and dim.

This meant, for one thing, that the eighth reflection he'd seen the first midnight had really been the fifteenth, since he'd only counted reflections of his face, as far as he could remember, and between every two of those there was a reflection of the back of his head. Oh, this mirror world, he decided, was fascinating! Or worlds, rather— a series of shells around him, like the crystal globes of Ptolemaic astronomy in which the stars and planets were set, going out in theory to infinity, and in each shell himself staring at himself in the next shell.

The way the heads got tinier intrigued him. He measured the distance between the two mirrors on the stairs —eight feet almost to the inch—and calculated that the eighth reflection of his face was therefore 116 feet away, as if it were peering back at him from a little attic window down the street, He was almost tempted to go to the roof and scan with his binoculars for such windows.

But since it was himself he was seeing, the eighth reflection was sizewise 232 feet away. He would have to scan for dwarfs. Most interesting!

It was delightful to think of all the different things his reflections could be doing, if each had the power to move around independently in the thin world of its crystal shell. Why, with all those shell-selves industriously occupied, Giles Nefandor could well become the world's most accomplished pianist, most knowledgeable field astronomer, and highest ranking of all chess grandmasters. The thought almost revived his dead ambitions—hadn't Lasker won the 1924 New York international tournament at 56!— while the charm of the speculation made him quite forget the menace of the black figure he'd now glimpsed three times.

Returning to reality somewhat reluctantly, he set himself to determine how many of his reflections he could see in practice rather than theory. He discovered that even with the best illumination, replacing all the dead bulbs in the wrought-iron chandelier, he could recognize at most only the ninth or perhaps the tenth reflection of his face. After that, his visage became a tiny indistinguishable ash-gray blank in the glass.

In reaching this conclusion, he also found that it was very difficult to count the reflections accurately. One or more would tend to get lost, or he'd lose count somewhere along the line. It was easiest to count the gilt mirror frames, since these stood in a close-packed row, like golden numeral ones—even though, for the tenth reflection of his face, say, this involved counting nineteen gilt ones, ten belonging to the mirror in front of him and nine to the mirror behind.

He wondered how he could have been so sure the first midnight that it was his eighth reflection which had shown the unpleasant alterations, and the seventh and sixth reflections on the two subsequent midnights. He decided that his shocked mind must have made a stabbing guess and that it very likely had been inaccurate—despite the instant uncertainty he'd felt. Next night he'd watch more carefully —and the fifth reflection would be easier to count.

He also discovered that although he could at most count ten reflections of his face, he could distinguish thirteen and perhaps fourteen reflections of a bright point of light —a pencil flashlight or even a candle-flame held close to his cheek. Those tinied candle-flames looked strangely like stars do in a cheap telescope. Odd.

He was eager to count more reflections than that—to break his record, as it were—and he even fetched his best pair of binoculars and stared into the mirror with them, using for light-point an inch of brightly flaming candle affixed to the top of the right-hand binocular tube. But as he'd feared, this was no help at all, magnification fading out the more distant light-points to nothing, like using too powerful an eyepiece on a small telescope.

He thought of making and testing out a periscope— candle attachment—but that seemed a touch over-elaborate. And in any case it was high time he got to bed— almost noon. He felt in remarkably good spirits—for the first time in years he had discovered a new thing in which to be interested. Reflectology mightn't be quite up to astronomy, musicology, or chess, but it was an elegant little science all the same. And the Mirror World was fascinating!—he looked forward excitedly to what he'd next see in it. If only the phenomena didn't stop!

It was perhaps his eagerness which got him between the stairway mirrors next night several seconds before the clock began to strike twelve. His early arrival, however, didn't inhibit the phenomena, as he suddenly feared might happen. They began on the clock's first twanging stroke and whatever may have happened on previous evenings, it was certainly the fifth reflection which was altered tonight. The figures were only about 70 feet away now, as he'd earlier calculated, and so considerably larger. His fifth reflected face was pale as ever, yet he fancied its expression was changing—but because it had gone more than halfway into eclipse behind the massed heads in front of it, he couldn't be sure.

And the black figure definitely was wearing a veil, although he still couldn't make out the features behind it. Yes, a veil . . . and long black gloves, one of which sleekly cased the slender arm outstretched to his shoulder

—for he suddenly realized that despite its height almost equal to his own, the figure was feminine.

A gust of fear hard to understand went through him at that discovery. As on the second night he wanted to strike out at the figure to prove its insubstantiality—smash the glass! But could that effect a figure 70 feet away? Would smashing the single glass in front of him smash all the nine panes he calculated still separated him from the figures in the Mirror World?

Perhaps it would—and then the black figure in the Mirror World could come straight out at him . . . now.

In any case the veiled figure, if she continued her approach, would be with him in five more nights.

Perhaps smashing the glass now would simply end the horrifying, fascinating phenomena—foil the figure for good. But did he want to do that?

As he asked himself that last question, the twelfth stroke came and the Black Lady in the fifth reflection vanished.

The rest of the night, while he played Tchaikovsky and studied the chess games of Vera Menchik, Lisa Lane, and Mrs. Piatigorsky, searching for hidden depths in them, he reviewed the Lives and Loves of Giles Nefandor. He discovered that the women in his life had been few, and those with whom he had become seriously entangled, or to whom he had done possible injury, fewer still. The half dozen candidates were all, so far as he knew, happily married and/or otherwise successful. This of course included his divorced wife, although she had often complained of him and his "hobbies."

On the whole, though romanticizing women, he had tended to run away from them, he concluded wryly. Perhaps the Dark Lady was a generalized woman, emblematic of the entire sex, come to be revenged on him for his faint-heartedness. His smile grew wryer. Perhaps her funeral costume was, anticipatorily, for him.

He thought, oh the human infatuation with guilt and retribution! The dread of and perhaps the desire for punishment! How ready we are to think others hate us!

During this search of his memory, the dark seed stirred several times—he seemed to be forgetting some one woman. But the seed refused to come clear of its burial until the clock struck its twelfth stroke next midnight, when just as the now clearly feminine figure in the fourth reflection vanished, he spoke the name, "Nina Fasinera."

That brought the buried incident—or rather all of it but one crucial part—back to him at once. It came back with that tigerish rush with which memory-lost small incidents and encounters will—one moment nonexistent, the next recalled with almost dizzying suddenness.

It had happened all of ten years ago, six years at least before his divorce, and he had only once met Miss Fasinera—a tall slender woman with black hair, bold hawklike features, slightly protruberant eyes, and rather narrow long mobile lips which the slim tip of her tongue was forever wetting. Her voice had been husky yet rapid and she had moved with a nervous pantherine grace, so that her heavy silk dress had hissed on her gaunt yet challenging figure.

Nina Fasinera had come to him, here at this house, on the pretext of asking his advice about starting a school of piano in a distant suburb across the city. She was an actress too, she had told him, but he had gathered she had not worked much in recent years—just as he had soon been guessing that her age was not much less than his own, the jet of her hair a dye, the taut smoothness of her facial skin astringents and an ivory foundation make-up, her youthful energy a product of will power—in short, that she was something of a fake (her knowledge of piano rudimentary, her acting a couple of seasons of summer stock and a few bit parts on Broadway), but a brave and gallant fake nonetheless.

Quite soon she had made it clean that she was somewhat more interested in him than in his advice and that she was ready—alert, on guard, dangerous, yet responsive— for any encounter with him, whether at a luncheon date a week in the future or here and now, on the instant.

It had been, he recalled, as if a duelist had lightly yet briskly brushed his cheek and lips with a thin leather glove. And yes, she *had* been wearing gloves, he remembered now of a sudden!—dark green ones edged with yellow, the same colors as her heavy silken dress.

He had been mightily attracted to her—strange how he had forgotten that taut nervous hour!—but he had just become re-reconciled with his wife for perhaps the dozenth time and there was about Nina Fasinera an avidity and a recklessness and especially an almost psychotic-seeming desperation which had frightened him or at least put him very much on guard. He recalled wondering if she took drugs.

So he had courteously yet most coolly and with infinite stubbornness refused all her challenges, which in the end had grown quite mocking, and he had shown her to the door and closed it on her.

And then the next day he had read in the paper of her suicide.

That was why he had forgotten the incident, he decided now—he had felt sharply guilty about it. Not that he thought that he possessed any fatal glamor, so that a woman would die at his rebuff, but that conceivably he had represented Nina Fasinera's last cast of the dice with destiny and he, not consciouly knowing what was at stake, had coldly told her, "You lose."

But there was something else he was forgetting—something about her death which his mind had suppressed even more tightly—he was certain of that. Glancing about uneasily, he stepped down onto the landing beneath the low-dipping chandelier and hurried down the rest of the stairs. He had just recalled that he had torn out the story of her death from a cheap tabloid and now he spent the rest of the night hunting for it among his haphazardly-filed papers. Toward dawn he discovered it, a ragged-edged browning thing tucked inside one of his additional copies of the Chopin nocturnes.

### FORMER BROADWAY ACTRESS
### DRESSES FOR OWN FUNERAL

Last night the glamorous Nina Fasinera, who was playing on Broadway as recently as three years ago, committed suicide by hanging, according to police Lieutenant Ben Davidow, in the room she rented at 1738 Waverly Place, Edgemont.

A purse with 87 cents in it lay on top of her dresser. She left no note or diary, however, though police are still searching. Despondency was the probable cause of Miss Fasinera's act, according to her landlady Elvira Winters, who discovered the body at 3 A.M.

"She was a charming tenant, always the lady, and very beautiful," Mrs. Winters said, "but lately she'd seemed

108

restless and unhappy. I'd let her get five weeks behind on her rent. Now who'll pay it?"

Before taking her life, the 39-year-old Miss Fasinera had dressed herself in a black silk cocktail gown with black accessories including a veil and long gloves. She had also pulled down the shades and turned on all the lights in the room. It was the glare of these lights through the transom which caused Mrs. Winters to enter the actress' small, high-ceilinged room by a duplicate key when there was no answer to her knocking.

There she saw Miss Fasinera's body hanging by a short length of clothesline from the ceiling light-fixture. A chair lay overturned nearby. In its plastic seat-cover Lieutenant Davidow later found impressions which matched the actress' spike heels. Dr. Leonard Belstrom estimated she had been dead for four hours when he examined the body at 4 A.M.

Mrs. Winters said, "She was hanging between the tall mirror on the closet door and the wide one on her dresser. She could almost have reached out and kicked them, if she could have kicked. I could see her in both of them, over and over, when I tried to lift her up, before I felt how cold she was. And then all those bright lights. It was horrible, but like the theater."

When Giles Nefandor finished reading the clipping, he nodded twice and stood frowning. Then he got out maps of the city and suburbs and measured the straight-line distance from the rooming house in Edgemont to his own place across the city, then used the scales on the maps to convert his measurements to miles.

Eleven and a half, it came out, as nearly as the limits of accuracy would make it.

Then he calculated the time that had elapsed since Nina Fasinera's death: ten years and one hundred and one days. From Mrs. Winters' statement, the distance between the mirrors between which she'd hanged herself had been about eight feet—the same distance as between the mirrors on his stairs. If she'd entered the Mirror World when she died and been advancing toward this house as she'd moved the last five nights—two reflections, or sixteen feet, each time—then in ten years and one hundred and one days she'd have traveled 60,058 feet.

That figured out to eleven miles and 1,978 feet.

Eleven and a half miles, or close to it.

He puzzled, almost idly, as to why a person could travel only such a short distance in the Mirror World each twenty-four hours. It must depend on the distance between the two mirrors of your departure and also on the two mirrors of your arrival. Perhaps you traveled one reflection for each day and one for each night. Perhaps his theory of shells like the Ptolemaic ones was true and in any shell there was only one door and you had to search to find it, as if you were traversing a maze; to find the right two doors in the crystal maze in twenty-four hours could be a most difficult task. And there must be all sorts of interlocking dimensions in the Mirror World—slow paths and fast ones: if you traveled between mirrors set on different stars, you might travel faster than light.

He wondered, again almost idly, why he had been chosen for this visitation and why of all women it should have been Nina Fasinera who had had the strength and the will to thread purposefully the glassy labyrinth for ten years. He was not so much frightened as awed—that an hour's meeting should lead to all these consequences. Could undying love grow in an hour? Or was it undying hate that had flowered? Had Nina Fasinera known about the Mirror World when she'd hanged herself?—he recalled now that one of the things she'd said lightly when she'd tried to storm his interest had been that she was a witch. And she would have known about the mirrors on his stairs matching those in her room—she'd seen them.

Next midnight when he saw the black figure in the third reflection, he instantly recognized Nina's pale gauntly lovely face behind the veil and wondered why he had not recognized it at least four nights before. Rather anxiously he glanced down toward her black-stockinged ankles, which were slender and unswollen, then quickly back to her face again. She was gazing at him gravely, perhaps with the ghost of a smile.

By now his own reflection was almost wholly eclipsed behind the ones in front of it. He could not even guess at his expression, nor did he want to. He had eyes only for Nina Fasinera. The impact of his years of unfelt loneliness shook him. He realized how desperately he had been wishing someone would search him out. The clock twanged on, swiftly marking time forever gone. Now he knew that he loved Nina Fasinera, had loved her since the one only hour they'd met. That was why he'd never stirred from this rotting house, why he'd prepared his mind for the Mirror World with chess-squares and singing wires and the stars. Since the hour they'd met . . . Except for color and the veil, her costume was the same she'd worn that fateful sixty minutes. If she'd only move, he thought, he'd faintly hear the hiss of the heavy silk through the five thick panes of glass remaining. If she'd only make that smile more certain . . .

The twelfth stroke twanged. This time he felt a terrible

pang of loss as her figure vanished, but it was swiftly replaced with a feeling of surety and faith.

For the next three of his nocturnal days, Giles Nefandor was happy and light-hearted. He played the piano music he loved best: Beethoven, Mozart, Chopin, Scriabin, Domenico Scarlatti. He played over the classic chess games of Nimzowitch, Alekhine, Capablanca, Emaneul Lasker, and Steinitz. He lovingly scanned his favorite celestial objects: the Beehive in Cancer, the Pleiades and Hyades, the Great Nebula in Orion's sword; he noticed new telescopic constellations and thought he saw the faintest crystal paths . . .

Occasionally his thoughts strayed eagerly yet guiltily, as if to forbidden fruit, to the mazy crystal corridors of the Mirror World, that secret diamond universe, and to his thousand wonderings about it: endless rooms and halls ceilinged and floored by transparency, and all the curious mirror-lost folk who lived adrift in them; piercingly sweet music; games of glass; revels and routs at a thousand levels; the tinkling of a million glittering chandeliers; diamond pathways to the farthest stars—

But he would always check these thoughts. There would be time enough for them, he felt certain. Experienced reality is always more satisfactory than imagination and illusion.

And often he would think of Nina and of the strangeness of their relationship: two atoms marked by one encounter and now drawn together among all the trillions of trillions of like atoms in the universe. Did it take ten years for love to grow, or only ten seconds? Both. But he checked these thoughts too—and struck the keys, or moved the men, or re-focused the 'scope.

There were moments of doubt and fear. Nina might be the incarnation of hate, the jet-black spider in the crystal web. Certainly she was the unknown, though he felt he knew her so well. There had been those early intimations of psychosis, of a pantherine restlessness. And there had been that first glimpse of his face, sick with horror . . . But they were moments only.

Before each of the three remaining midnights he dressed with unusual care: the black suit newly brushed, the white shirt fresh, the narrow black necktie carefully knotted. It pleased him to think that he had not had to change the color of his suit to match that of her dress.

The first of the three midnights he was almost certain of her smile.

The next midnight he was sure of it. Now both figures were in the first reflection and he could see his own face again, scarce four feet away. He too was smiling gravely —the horror was gone.

Nina's black-gloved hand resting on his shoulder, the black fingertips touching his white collar, now seemed a lover's gesture.

The night after that the wind came back at last, blowing with more and more violence, although there were no clouds, so that the stars flickered and streamed impossibly in his 'scopes. The gale seemed to fasten on and shake their beams like crystal stalks. The sky was granular with wind. He could not remember such a blow. By eleven it had almost driven him from the roof, but he stuck it out although the wind increased in frenzy.

Instead of daunting, it filled him with a terrific excitement. He felt he could leap into the air and be blown light-swift anywhere he willed in the diamond-dazzling cosmos —except that he had another rendezvous.

When he finally went inside, shaking with the cold, and took off his fleece-lined coat, he became aware of a rhythmic crunching and crashing below, with rather long intervals between.

When he went down the stairs, they were dark and the crashes were louder. He realized that the great chandelier above the landing must be swinging so far that it was hitting the lead-webbed windows beyond, breaking their remaining panes—and had long since burst all the electric globes it carried.

He felt his way down by the wall, keeping close to it to avoid the chandelier's murderous swings. His fingers touched absolute smoothness—glass. Then the glass *rippled* for an instant, tingling his fingers, and he heard husky irregular breathing and the hissing of heavy silk. Then slender arms were around him and a woman's slim body was pressed against his and hungry lips met his lips, first through a faintly astringent, dryish, tormenting tantalizing veil, then flesh to flesh. He could feel under his hands the ribbed smoothness of heavy silk and of pliant, lightly fleshed ribs under that.

All in utter darkness and pandemonium. Almost drowned in the latter, midnight's last strokes were twanging.

A hand moved up his back and suede-cased fingers lightly brushed his neck. As the last strokes twanged, one of the fingers turned hard and stiff and cruel and dug under his collar so that it caught him like a hook by the collar and the tightly-knitted tie the collar covered. It wrenched him into the air. A terrible pain stabbed at the base of his skull, then filled it to bursting.

It was four days before the policeman who nightly patrolled beyond the gate discovered by a stab of his flash-

114

light the body of Giles Nefandor—whom he knew by sight, though never a sight like this!—hanging from the wrought iron chandelier above the landing strewn with glassy shards. It might have been longer than four days, except that a chessplayer across the city, contesting a correspondence game with the well-known recluse, spurred the police into action when the move on his last postcard had gone ten days unanswered. His first queries were ignored, but an evening phone call got action.

The policeman reported back the unpleasant condition of the body, the black, hooked, wrought-iron chandelier-finger thrust under the noose of collar and tie, and the glass shards, and several other matters.

He never did report what he saw in one of the two mirrors on the stairs when he looked at it closely, his powerful flash beside his chest as his wristwatch signaled midnight. There was a stack of reflections of his own shocked, sharply shadowed face. But in the fourth reflection there were momentarily two figures, hand in hand, looking back toward him over their shoulders—and smiling impishly at him, he thought. The one figure was that of Giles Nefandor, though looking more youthful than he recalled seeing him in recent years. The other was that of a lady in black, the upper half of her face veiled.

# THE NUMBER OF THE BEAST

"I wish," said the Young Captain, police chief of High Chicago, the turbulent satellite that hangs over the meridian of the midwestern groundside city, "I wish that sometimes the telephathic races of the Galaxy weren't such consistent truth-tellers and silence-keepers."

"Your four suspects are all telepaths?" the Old Lieutenant asked.

"Yes. I also wish I had more than half an hour to decide which one to accuse. But Earthside has muscled into the case and the pressure is on. If I can't reason it out, I must make a guess. A bare half-hour they give me."

"Then perhaps you shouldn't waste it with a pensioned-off old louey."

The Young Captain shook his head decisively. "No. You think. You have time to now."

The Old Lieutenant smiled. "Sometimes I wish I hadn't. And I doubt if I can give you any special angles on telepaths, Jim. It's true I've lately been whiling away the time on informal study of alien thought systems with Khla-Khla the Martian, but—"

"I didn't come to you looking for a specialist on telepathy," the Young Captain asserted sharply.

"Very well then, Jim. You know what you're doing. Let's hear your case. And give me background. I don't keep up with the news."

The Young Captain looked skeptical. "Everyone in High Chicago has heard about the murder—not two furlongs from here—of the representative of the Arcturian peace party."

"I haven't," the Old Lieutenant said. "Who are the Arcturians? I tell you, for an oldster like me, the Now is just one more historical period. Better consult someone else, Jim."

"No. The Arcturians are the first non-related humanoid race to turn up in the Galaxy. Non-related to Earth humans, that is, True, they have three eyes, and six fingers on each hand, but they are hairless mammalian bipeds just the same. One of their females is the current burlesque sensation of the Star and Garter."

"The police found that a good spot to keep their eyes on in my day too," the Old Lieutenant recalled, nodding. "Are the Arcturians telepaths?"

"No. I'll come to the telepathy angle later. The Arcturians are split into two parties: those who want to enter the Commerce Union and open their planets to alien starships, including Earth's—the peace party, in short—and those who favor a policy of strict non-intercourse which, as far as we know, always ultimately leads to war. The war party is rather the stronger of the two. Any event may tip the balance."

"Such as a representative of the peace party coming quietly to Earth and getting himself bumped before he even gets down from High Chicago?"

"Exactly. It looks bad, Sean. It looks as if *we* wanted war. The other member peoples of the Commerce Union

are skeptical enough already about the ultimate peace-
fulness of Earth's intentions toward the whole Galaxy.
They look on the Arcturian situation as a test. They say
that we accepted the Polarians and Antareans and all the
rest as equals simply because they *are* so different from
us in form and culture—it's easy to admit theoretical
equality with a bumblebee, say, and then perhaps do him
dirt afterward.

"But, our galactic critics ask, will Earthmen be so
ready or willing to admit equality with a humanoid race?
It's sometimes harder, you know, to agree that your own
brother is a human being than to grant the title to an
anonymous peasant on the other side of the globe. They
say—I continue to speak for our galactic critics—that
Earthmen will openly work for peace with Arcturus while
secretly sabotaging it."

"Including murder."

"Right, Sean. So unless we can pin this crime on aliens
—best of all on extremists in the Arcturian war party
(something I believe but can in no way prove)—the
rumor will go through the Union that Earth wants war,
while the Arcturian Earth-haters will have everything
their own way."

"Leave off the background, Jim. How was the murder
done?"

Permitting himself a bitter smile, the Young Captain
said wistfully, "With the whole Galaxy for a poison cabi-
net and a weapon shop, with almost every means available
of subtle disguise, of sudden approach and instantaneous
getaway—everything but a time machine, and some crook
will come along with that any day now—the murder had
to be done with a blunt instrument and by one of four

aliens domiciled in the same caravansary as the Arcturian peace-party man.

"There's something very ugly, don't you think, in the vision of a blackjack gripped by the tentacle of an octopoid or in the pincers of a black Martian? To be frank, Sean, I'd rather the killer had been fancier in his *modus operandi*. It would have let me dump the heavy end of the case in the laps of the science boys."

"I was always grateful myself when I could invoke the physicists," the Old Lieutenant agreed. "It's marvelous what colored lights and the crackle of Geiger counters do to take the pressure off a plain policeman. These four aliens you mention are the telepaths?"

"Right, Sean. Shady characters, too, all four of them, criminals for hire, which makes it harder. And each of them takes the typical telepath point of view—Almighty, how it exasperates me! That we ought to *know* which one of them is guilty without asking questions! They know well enough that Earthmen aren't telepathic, but still they hide behind the lofty pretense that every intelligent inhabitant of the Cosmos *must* be telepathic.

"If you come right out and tell them that your mind is absolutely deaf-dumb-and-blind to the thoughts of others, they act as if you'd made a dreadful social blunder and they cover up for you by pretending not to have heard you. Talk about patronizing—! Why, they're like a woman who is forever expecting you to know what it is she's angry about without ever giving you a hint what it is. They're like—"

"Now, now, I've dealt with a few telepaths in my time, Jim. I take it that the other prong of your dilemma is that if you officially accuse one of them, *and you hit it right,* than he will up and confess like a good little animal, using the ritual of speech to tell you who commissioned the murder and all the rest of it, and everything will be rosy.

"But *if you hit it wrong,* it will be a mortal insult to his whole race—to all telepaths, for that matter—and there will be whole solar systems moving to resign from the Union and all manner of other devils to pay. Because, continuing the telepath's fiction, that you are a telepath yourself, you must have known he was innocent and yet you accused him."

"Most right, Sean," the Young Captain admitted ruefully. "As I said at the beginning, truth-tellers and silence-keepers—intellectual prigs, all of them! Refusing to betray each other's thoughts to a non-telepath, I can understand that—though just one telepathic stoolpigeon would make police work ten mountains easier. But all these other lofty idealistic fictions do get my goat! If I were running the Union—".

"Jim, your time is running short. I take it you want help in deciding which one to accuse. That is, if you *do* decide to chance it rather than shut your mouth, lose face and play for time."

"I've got to chance it, Sean—Earthside demands it. But as things stand, I'll be backing no better than a three-to-one shot. For you see, Sean, every single suspect of the four is just as suspect as the others. In my book, they're four equally bad boys."

"Sketch me your suspects then, quickly." The Old Lieutenant closed his eyes.

"There's Tlik-Tcha the Martian," the Young Captain began, ticking them off on his fingers. "A nasty black beetle, that one. Held his breath for twenty minutes and then belched it in my face. Kept printing 'No Comment' white-on-black on his chest to whatever I asked him. In Garamond type!"

"Cheer up, Jim. It might have been Rustic Capitals. Next."

"Hlilav the Antarean multibrach. Kept gently waving his tentacles all through the interrogation—I thought he was trying to hypnotize me! Then it occurred to me he might be talking in code, but the interpreter said no. At the end, he gives a long insulting whistle, like some shameless swish. Whistle didn't signify anything either, the interpreter said, beyond a polite wish for my serenity.

"Third customer was Fa the Rigelian composite. Took off a limb—real, of course, not artificial—and kept fiddling with it while I shot questions at him. I could hardly keep my mind on what I was saying—expected him to take his head off next! He did that too, just as he started back to his cell."

"Telepaths can surely be exasperating," the Old Lieutenant agreed. "I always had great trouble in keeping in mind what a boring business a vocal interview must be to them—very much as if a man, quite capable of speech, should insist on using a pencil and paper to conduct a conversation with you, with perhaps the further proviso that you print your remarks stylishly. Your fourth suspect, Jim?"

"Hrohrakak the Polarian centipedal. He reared up in a great question-mark bend when I addressed him—looked very much like a giant cobra covered with thick black fur. Kept chattering to himself too, very low—interpreter said he was saying over and over again, 'Oh, All-father, when will this burden be lifted from me?' Halfway through, he reaches out a little black limb to Donovan to give him what looks like a pretty pink billiard ball."

"Oh, naughty, naughty," the Old Leiutenant observed, shaking his head while he smiled. "So these are your four suspects, Jim? The four rather gaudy racehorses of whom you must back one?"

"They are. Each of them had opportunity. Each of them has a criminal reputation and might well have been hired to do the murder—either by extremists in the Arcturian war party or by some other alien organization hostile to Earth—such as the League of the Beasts with its pseudo-religious mumbo-jumbo."

"I don't agree with you about the League, but don't forget our own bloody-minded extremists," the Old Lieutenant reminded him. "There are devils among us too, Jim."

"True, Sean. But whoever paid for this crime, any one of the four might have been his agent. For to complete the problem and tie it up in a Gordian knot a yard thick, each one of my suspects has recently and untraceably received a large sum of money—enough so that, in each case, it might well have paid for murder."

Leaning forward the Old Lieutenant said, "So? Tell me about that, Jim."

"Well, you know the saying that the price of a being's life anywhere in the Galaxy is one thousand of whatever happens to be the going unit of big money. And as you know, it's not too bad a rule of thumb. In this case, the unit is gold martians, which are neither gold nor backed by Mar's bitter little bureaucracy, but—"

"I know! You've only minutes left, Jim. What were the exact amounts?"

"Hlilav the Antarean multibrach had received 1024 gold martians, Hrohrakak the Polarian centipedal 1000 gold martians, Fa the Rigelian composite 1728 gold martians, Tlik-Tcha the Martian coleopteroid 666 gold martians."

"Ah—" the Old Lieutenant said very soft. "The number of the beast."

"Come again, Sean?"

" 'Here is wisdom,' " quoted the Old Lieutenant, still speaking very softly. " 'Let him that hath understanding count the number of the beast: for it is the number of a man'; *Revelation,* Jim, the last book in the Bible."

"I know that," the Young Captain burst out excitedly. "I also know the next words, if only because they're a favorite with numerology crackpots—of whom I see quite a few at the station. The next words are: 'and his number is Six hundred threescore and six.' Almighty, that's Tlik-Tcha's—that's the number of his gold martians! And we've always known that the League of Beasts got some of its mumbo-jumbo from Earth, so why not from its Bible? Sean, you clever old devil, I'm going to play your hunch." The Young Captain sprang up. "I'm going back to the station and have the four of them in and accuse Tlik-Tcha to his face."

The Old Lieutenant lifted a hand. "One moment, Jim," he said sharply. "You're to go back to the station, to be sure, and have the four of them in, yes—but you're to accuse Fa the Rigelian."

The Young Captain almost sat down again, involuntarily. "But that doesn't make sense, Sean," he protested. "Fa's number is 1728. That doesn't fit your clue. It's not the number of the beast."

"Beasts have all sorts of numbers, Jim," the Old Lieutenant said. "The one you want is 1728."

"But your reason, Sean? Give me your reason."

"No. There's no time and you mightn't believe me if I did. You asked for my advice and I've given it to you. Accuse Fa the Rigelian."

"But—"

"That's all, Jim."

Minutes later, the Young Captain was still feeling the slow burn of his exasperation, though he was back at the station and the moment of decision weighed sickeningly upon him. What a fool he'd been, he told himself savagely, to waste his time on such an old dodderer! The nerve of the man, giving out with advice—orders, practically!—that he refused to justify, behaving with the whimsicality, the stubbornness—yes, the insolence!—that only the retired man can afford.

He scanned the four alien faces confronting him across the station desk—Tlik-Tcha's like a section of ebon bowling ball down to the three deeply recessed perceptors, Hrohrakak's a large black floormop faintly quivering, Fa's pale and humanoid, but oversize, like an emperor's death mask, Hlilav's a cluster of serially blinking eyes and greenish jowls. He wished he could toss them all in a bag and reach in—wearing an armor-plated glove—and pick one.

The room stank of disinfectants and unwashed alienity —the familiar reek of the oldtime police station greatly diversified. The Young Captain felt the sweat trickling down his flushed forehead. He opened wide the louver behind him and the hum of the satellite's central concourse poured in. It didn't help the atmosphere, but for a moment he felt less constricted.

Then he scanned the four faces once more and the deadline desperation was back upon him. *Pick a number,* he thought, *any number from one to two thousand. Grab a face. Trust to luck. Sean's a stubborn old fool, but the boys always said he had the damnedest luck . . .*

His finger stabbed out. "In the nexus of these assembled minds," he said loudly, "I publish the truth I share with yours, Fa—"

That was all he had time to get out. At his first movement, the Rigelian sprang up, whipped off his head and hurled it straight toward the center of the open louver.

But if the Young Captain had been unready for thought, he was more than keyed up for action. He snagged the head as it shot past, though he fell off his chair in doing it. The teeth snapped once, futilely. Then a tiny voice from the head spoke the words he'd been praying for; "Let the truth that our minds share be published forth. But first, please, take me back to my breath source . . ."

Next day, the Old Lieutenant and the Young Captain talked it all over.

"So you didn't nab Fa's accomplices in the concourse?" the Old Lieutenant asked.

"No, Sean, they got clean away—as they very likely would have, with Fa's head, if they'd managed to lay their hands on it. Fa wouldn't rat on them."

"But otherwise our fancy-boy killer confessed in full? Told the whole story, named his employers, and provided the necessary evidence to nail them and himself once and for all?"

"He did indeed. When one of those telepath characters does talk, it's a positive pleasure to hear him. He makes it artistic, like an oration from Shakespeare. But now, sir, I want to ask the question you said you didn't have time to answer yesterday—though I'll admit I'm asking it with a little different meaning than when I asked it first. You gave me a big shock then and I'll admit that I'd never have gone along and followed your advice blind the way I did, except that I had nothing else to go on, and I *was* impressed with that Bible quotation you had so pat —until you told me it didn't mean what it seemed to!

"But I *did* follow your advice, and it got me out of one of the worst jams I've ever been in—with a pat on the back from Earthside to boot! So now let me ask you, Sean, in the name of all that's holy, how did you know so surely which one of the four it was?"

"I didn't know, Jim. It's more accurate to say I guessed."

"You old four-flusher! Do you mean to say you just played a lucky hunch?"

"Not quite, Jim. It was a guess, all right, but an educated guess. It all lay in the numbers, of course, the numbers of gold martians, the numbers of our four beasts. Tlick-Tcha's 666 did strongly indicate that he was in the employ of the League of the Beasts, for I understand they are great ones on symbolic actions and like to ring in the number 666 whenever they can. But that gets us just nowhere—the League, though highly critical of most Earthmen, has never shown itself desirous of fomenting interstellar war.

"Hrohrakak's 1000 would indicate that he was receiving money from some organization of Earthmen, or from some alien source that happens also to use the decimal system. Anyone operating around Sol would be apt to use the decimal system. Hrohrakak's 1000 points in no one direction.

"Now as to Hlilav's 1024—that number is the tenth

power of two. As far as I know, no natural species of being uses the binary system. However, it is the rule with robots. The indications are that Hlilav is working for the Interstellar Brotherhood of Free Business Machines or some like organization, and, as we both know, the robots are not ones to pound the war drums or touch off the war fuses, for they are always the chief sufferers.

"That leaves Fa's 1728. Jim, the first thing you told me about the Arcturians was that they were hexadactylic bipeds. Six fingers on one hand means 12 on two—and almost a mortal certainty that the beings so equipped by nature will be using the duodecimal system, in many ways the most convenient of all. In the duodecimal system, 'one thousand' is not 10 times 10 times 10, but 12 times 12 times 12—which comes out as 1728 exactly in our decimal system.

"As you said, 'one thousand' of the going unit is the price of a being's life. Someone paid 'one thousand' gold martians by an Arcturian would have 1728 in his pocket according to our count.

"The size of Fa's purse seemed to me an odds-on indication that he was in the pay of the Arcturians war party. Incidentally, he must have felt very smart getting that extra 728—a more principled beast-criminal would have scorned to profit from a mere difference in numerical systems."

The Young Captain took some time before he answered. He smiled incredulously more than once, and once he shook his head.

Finally he said, "And you asked me to go ahead, Sean, and make my accusation, with no more indication than that?"

"It worked for you, didn't it?" the Old Lieutenant

countered briskly. "And as soon as Fa started to confess, you must have known I was right beyond any possibility of doubt. Telepaths are always truth-tellers."

The Young Captain shot him a very strange look.

"It couldn't be, Sean—?" he said softly. "It couldn't be that you're a telepath yourself? That that's the alien thought system you've been studying with your Martian witch doctor?"

"If it were," the Old Lieutenant replied, "I'd tell—" He stopped. He twinkled. "Or would I?"

# THE MIND SPIDER

Hour and minute hand of the odd little gray clock stood almost at midnight, Horn Time, and now the second hand, driven by the same tiny, invariable radioactive pulses, was hurrying to overtake them. Morton Horn took note. He switched off his book, puffed a brown cigarette alight, and slumped back gratefully against the saddle-shaped forcefield which combined the sensations of swansdown and laced rawhide.

When all three hands stood together, he flicked the switch of a small black cubical box in his smock pocket. A look of expectancy came into his pleasant, swarthy face, as if he were about to receive a caller, although the door had not spoken.

With the flicking of the switch a curtain of brainwave static surrounding his mind vanished. Unnoticed while present, because it was a meaningless thought-tone—a kind of mental gray—the vanishing static left behind a great inward silence and emptiness. To Morton it was as if his mind were crouched on a mountainpeak in infinity.

"Hello, Mort. Are we first?"

A stranger in the room could not have heard those words, yet to Mort they were the cheeriest and friendliest greeting imaginable—words clear as crystal without any of the air-noise or bone-noise that blurs ordinary speech, and they sounded like chocolate tastes.

"Guess so, Sis," his every thought responded, "unless the others have started a shaded contact at their end."

His mind swiftly absorbed a vision of his sister Grayl's studio upstairs, just as it appeared to her. A corner of the work table, littered with air-brushes and cans of dye and acid. The easel, with one half-completed film for the multi-level picture she was spraying, now clouded by cigarette smoke. In the foreground, the shimmery gray curve of her skirt and the slim, competent beauty of her hands, so close—especially when she raised the cigarette to puff it—that they seemed his own. The feathery touch of her clothes on her skin. The sharp cool tingly tone of her muscles. In the background, only floor and cloudy sky, for the glastic walls of her studio did not refract.

The vision seemed a ghostly thing at first, a shadowy projection against the solid walls of his own study. But as the contact between their minds deepened, it grew more real. For a moment the two visual images swung apart and stood side by side, equally real, as if he were trying to focus one with each eye. Then for another moment his room became the ghost room and Grayl's the real one—as if he had become Grayl. He raised the cigarette in her hand to her lips and inhaled the pleasant fumes, milder than those of his own *rompe-pecho*. Then he savored the two at once and enjoyed the mental blending of her Virginia cigarette with his own Mexican "chestbreaker."

From the depths of her . . . his . . . *their* mind Grayl laughed at him amiably.

"Here now, don't go sliding into *all* of me!" she told him. "A girl ought to be allowed some privacy."

"Should she?" he asked teasingly.

"Well, at least leave me my fingers and toes! What if Fred had been visiting me?"

"I knew he wasn't," Morton replied. "You know, Sis, I'd never invade your body while you were with your non-telepathic sweetheart."

"Nonsense, you'd love to, you old hedonist!—and I don't think I'd grudge you the experience—especially if at the same time you let me be with your lovely Helen! But now please get out of me. *Please*, Morton."

He retreated obediently until their thoughts met only at the edges. But he had noticed something strangely skittish in her first reaction. There had been a touch of hysteria in even the laughter and banter and certainly in the final plea. And there had been a knot of something like fear under her breastbone. He questioned her about it. Swiftly as the thoughts of one person, the mental dialogue spun itself out.

"Really afraid of me taking control of you, Grayl?"

"Of course not, Mort! I'm as keen for control-exchange experiments as any of us, especially when I exchange with a man. But . . . we're so exposed, Mort—it sometimes bugs me."

"How do you mean exactly?"

"You know, Mort. Ordinary people are protected. Their minds are walled in from birth, and behind the walls it may be stuffy but it's very safe. So safe that they don't even realize that there *are* walls . . . that there are frontiers of mind as well as frontiers of matter . . . and that things can get at you across those frontiers."

"What sort of things? Ghosts? Martians? Angels? Evil spirits? Voices from the Beyond? Big bad black static-clouds?" His response was joshing. "You know how flatly we've failed to establish any contacts in those directions. As mediums we're a howling failure. We've never got so much as a hint of any telepathic mentalities save our own. Nothing in the whole mental universe but silence and occasional clouds of noise—static—*and* the sound of distant Horns, if you'll pardon the family pun."

"I know Mort, but we're such a tiny young cluster of mind, and the universe is an awfully big place and there's a chance of some awfully queer things existing in it. Just yesterday I was reading an old Russian novel from the Years of Turmoil and one of the characters said something that my memory photographed. Now where did I tuck it away?—No, keep out of my files, Mort! I've got it anyway—here it is."

, A white oblong bobbed up in her mind. Morton read the black print on it.

"We always imagine eternity (it said) as something beyond our conception, something vast, vast! But why must it be vast? Instead of all that, what if it's one little room, like a bathhouse in the country, black and grimy and spiders in every corner, and that's all eternity is? I sometimes fancy it like that."

"Brrr!" Morton thought, trying to make the shiver comic for Grayl's sake. "Those old White and Red Russkies certainly had black minds! Andreyev? Dostoyevsky?"

"Or Svidrigailov, or some name like that. But it wasn't the book that bothered me. It was that about an hour ago I switched off my static box to taste the silence and for the first time in my life I got the feeling there was something nasty and alien in infinity and that it was watching me, just like those spiders in the bathhouse. It had been asleep for centuries but now it was waking up. I switched on my box *fast!*"

"Ho-ho! The power of suggestion! Are you sure that Russian wasn't named Svengali, dear self-hypnosis-susceptible sister?"

"Stop poking fun! It was *real*, I tell you."

"Real? How? Sounds like mood-reality to me. Here, stop being so ticklish and let me get a close-up."

He started mock-forcibly to explore her memories, thinking that a friendly mental roughhouse might be what she needed, but she pushed away his thought-tendrils with a panicky and deathly-serious insistence. Then he saw her decisively stub out her cigarette and he felt a sudden secretive chilling of her feelings.

"It's all really nothing, Mort," she told him briskly. "Just a mood, I guess, like you say. No use bothering a family conference with a mood, no matter how black and devilish."

"Speaking of the devil and his cohorts, here we are! May we come in?" The texture of the interrupting thought was bluff and yet ironic, highly individual—suggesting not chocolate but black coffee. Even if Mort and Grayl had not been well acquainted with its tone and rhythms, they would have recognized it as that of a third person. It was as if a third dimension had been added to the two of their shared mind. They knew it immediately.

"Make yourself at home, Uncle Dean," was the welcome Grayl gave him. "Our minds are yours."

"Very cozy indeed," the newcomer responded with a show of gruff amusement. "I'll do as you say, my dear. Good to be in each other again." They caught a glimpse of scudding ragged clouds patching steel-blue sky above to gray-green forest below—their uncle's work as a ranger kept him up in his flyabout a good deal of the day.

"Dean Horn coming in," he announced with a touch of formality and then immediately added, "Nice tidy little mental parlor you've got, as the fly said to the spider."

"Uncle Dean!—what made you think of spiders?" Grayl's question was sharply anxious.

"Haven't the faintest notion, my dear. Maybe recalling the time we took turns mind-sitting with Evelyn until she got over her infant fear of spiders. More likely just reflecting a thought-flicker from your own unconscious or Morton's. Why the fear-flurry?"

But just then a fourth mind joined them—resinous in flavor like Greek wine. "Hobart Horn coming in." They saw a ghostly laboratory, with chemical apparatus.

Then a fifth—sweet-sour apple-tasting. "Evelyn Horn coming in. Yes, Grayl, late as usual—thirty-seven seconds by Horn Time. I didn't miss your cluck-cluck thought." The newcomer's tartness was unmalicious. They glimpsed the large office in which Evelyn worked, the microtypewriter and rolls of her correspondence tape on her desk. "But—bright truth!—someone always has to be last," she continued. "And I'm working overtime. Always make a family conference, though. Afterwards will you take control of me, Grayl, and spell me at this typing for a while? I'm really fagged—and I don't want to leave my body on automatic too long. It gets hostile on automatic and hurts to squeeze back into. How about it, Grayl?"

"I will," Grayl promised, "but don't make it a habit. I don't know what your administrator would say if he knew you kept sneaking off two thousand miles to my studio to smoke cigarettes—and get *my* throat raw for me!"

"All present and accounted for," Mort remarked. "Evelyn, Grayl, Uncle Dean, Hobart, and myself—the whole damn family. Would you care to share my day's experiences first? Pretty dull armchair stuff, I warn you. Or shall we make it a five-dimensional free-for-all? A Quintet for Horns? Hey, Evelyn, quit directing four-letter thoughts at the chair!"

With that the conference got underway. Five minds that were in a sense one mind, because they were wide open to each other, and in another sense twenty-five minds, because there were five sensory-memory set-ups available for each individual. Five separate individuals, some of them thousands of miles apart, each viewing a different sector of the world of the First Global Democracy. Five separate visual landscapes—study, studio, laboratory, office, and the cloud-studded openness of the upper air—all of them existing in one mental space, now superimposed on each other, now replacing each other, now jostling each other as two ideas may jostle in a single non-telepathic mind. Five varying auditory landscapes —the deep throb of the vanes of Dean's flyabout making the dominant tone, around which the other noises wove counterpoint. In short, five complete sensory pictures, open to mutual inspection.

Five different ideational set-ups too. Five concepts of truth and beauty and honor, of good and bad, of wise and foolish, and of all the other so-called abstractions with which men and women direct their lives—all different, yet all vastly more similar than such concepts are among the non-telepathic, who can never really share them. Five different ideas of life, jumbled together like dice in a box.

And yet there was no confusion. The dice were educated. The five minds slipped into and out of each other with the practiced grace and courtesy of diplomats at a tea. For these daily conferences had been going on ever since Grandfather Horn first discovered that he could communicate mentally with his children. Until then he had not known that he was a telepathic mutant, for before his children were born there had been no other minds with which he could communicate—and the strange mental silence, disturbed from time to time by clouds of mental static, had even made him fear that he was psychotic. Now Grandfather Horn was dead, but the conferences went on between the members of the slowly widening circle of his lineal descendants—at present only five in number, although the mutation appeared to be a partial dominant. The conferences of the Horns were still as secret as the earliest ones had been. The First Global Democracy was still ignorant that telepathy was a long-established fact—among the Horns. For the Horns believed that jealousy and suspicion and savage hate would be what they would get from the world if it ever became generally known that, by the chance of mutated heredity, they possessed a power which other men could never hope for. Or else they would be exploited as all-weather and interplanetary "radios." So to the outside world, including even their non-telepathic husbands and wives, sweethearts and friends, they were just an ordinary group of blood relations—no more "psychic" certainly than any group of close-knit brothers and sisters and cousins. They had something of a reputation of being a family of "daydreamers"—that was about all. Beyond enriching their personalities and experience, the Horns' telepathy was no great advantage to them. They could not read the minds of animals and other humans and they seemed to have no powers whatever of clairvoyance, clairaudience, telekinesis, or foreseeing the future or past. Their telepathic power was, in short, simply like having a private, all-senses family telephone.

The conference—it was much more a hyper-intimate gabfest—proceeded.

"My static box bugged out for a few ticks this morning," Evelyn remarked in the course of talking over the trivia of the past twenty-four hours.

The static boxes were an invention of Grandfather Horn. They generated a tiny cloud of meaningless brain waves. Without such individual thought-screens, there was too much danger of complete loss of individual personality —once Grandfather Horn had "become" his infant daughter as well as himself for several hours and the unfledged mind had come close to being permanently lost in its own subconscious. The static boxes provided a mental wall behind which a mind could safely grow and function, similar to the wall by which ordinary minds are apparently always enclosed.

In spite of the boxes, the Horns shared thoughts and emotions to an amazing degree. Their mental togetherness was as real and as mysterious—and as incredible—as thought itself . . . and thought is the original angel-cloud dancing on the head of a pin. Their present conference was as warm and intimate and tart as any actual family gathering in one actual room around one actual table. Five minds, joined together in the vast mental darkness that shrouds *all* minds. Five minds hugged together for comfort and safety in the infinite mental loneliness that pervades the cosmos.

Evelyn continued, "Your boxes were all working, of course, so I couldn't get your thoughts—just the blurs of your boxes like little old dark gray stars. But this time it gave me a funny uncomfortable feeling, like a spider crawling down my—Grayl! Don't *feel* so wildly! What *is* it?"

Then . . . just as Grayl started to think her answer . . . *something crept from the vast mental darkness and infinite cosmic loneliness surrounding the five minds of the Horns.*

Grayl was the first to notice. Her panicky thought had the curling too-keen edge of hysteria. "There are six of us now! There should only be five, but there are six. Count! Count, I tell you! Six!"

To Mort it seemed that a gigantic spider was racing across the web of their thoughts. He felt Dean's hands grip convulsively at the controls of his flyabout. He felt Evelyn's slave-body freeze at her desk and Hobart grope out blindly so that a piece of apparatus fell with a crystalline tinkle. As if they had been sitting together at dinner and had suddenly realized that there was a sixth place set and a tall figure swathed in shadows sitting at it. A figure that to Mort exuded an overpowering taste and odor of brass—a sour metallic stench.

And then that figure spoke. The greater portion of the intruder's thought was alien, unintelligible, frightening in its expression of an unearthly power and an unearthly hunger.

The understandable portion of its speech seemed to be in the nature of a bitter and coldly menacing greeting, insofar as references and emotional sense could be at all determined.

"I, the Mind Spider as you name me—the deathless one, the eternally exiled, the eternally imprisoned—or so his overconfident enemies suppose—coming in."

Mort saw the danger almost too late—and he was the first to see it. He snatched toward the static box in his smock.

In what seemed no more than an instant he saw the shadow of the intruder darken the four other minds, saw them caught and wrapped in the intruder's thoughts, just as a spider twirls a shroud around its victims, saw the black half-intelligible thoughts of the intruder scuttle toward him with blinding speed, felt the fanged impact of indomitable power, felt his own will fail.

There was a click. By a hairsbreadth his fingers had carried out their mission. Around his mind the neutral gray wall was up and—Thank the Lord!—it appeared that the intruder could not penetrate it.

Mort sat there gasping, shaking, staring with the dull eyes of shock. Direct mental contact with the utterly inhuman—with *that* sort of inhumanity—is not something that can be lightly brushed aside or ever forgotten. It makes a wound. For minutes afterwards a man cannot think at all.

And the brassy stench lingered tainting his entire consciousness—a stench of Satanic power and melancholy.

When he finally sprang up, it was not because he had thought things out but because he heard a faint sound behind him and knew with a chilling certainty that it meant death.

It was Grayl. She was carrying an airbrush as if it were a gun. She had kicked off her shoes. Poised there in the doorway she was the incarnation of taut stealthiness, as if she had sloughed off centuries of civilization in seconds of time, leaving only the primeval core of the jungle killer.

But it was her face that was the worst, and the most

revealing. Pale and immobile as a corpse's—almost. But the little more left over from the "almost" was a spiderish implacability, the source of which Mort knew only too well.

She pointed the airbrush at his eyes. His sidewise twist saved them from the narrow pencil of oily liquid that spat from the readjusted nozzle, but a little splashed against his hand and he felt the bite of acid. He lunged toward her, ducking away from the spray as she whipped it back toward him. He caught her wrist, bowled into her, and carried her with him to the floor.

She dropped the airbrush and fought—with teeth and claws like a cat, yet with this horrible difference that it was not like an animal lashing out instinctively but like an animal listening for orders and obeying them.

Suddenly she went limp. The static from his box had taken effect. He made doubly sure by switching on hers.

She was longer than he had been in recovering from the shock, but when she began to speak it was with a rush, as if she already realized that every minute was vital.

"We've got to stop the others, Mort, before they let it out. The . . . the Mind Spider, Mort! It's been imprisoned for eons, for cosmic ages. First floating in space, then in the Antarctic, where its prison spiralled to Earth. Its enemies . . . really its judges . . . *had* to imprison it, because it's something that can't be killed. I can't make you understand just why they imprisoned it—" (Her face went a shade grayer) "—you'd have to experience the creature's thoughts for that—but it had to do with the perversion and destruction of the life-envelopes of more than one planet."

Even under the stress of horror, Mort had time to realize how strange it was to be listening to Grayl's words instead of her thoughts. They never used words except when ordinary people were present. It was like acting in a play. Suddenly it occurred to him that they would never be able to share thoughts again. Why, if their static boxes were to fail for a few seconds, as Evelyn's had this morning . . .

"That's where it's been," Grayl continued, "locked in the heart of the Antarctic, dreaming its centuries-long dreams of escape and revenge, waking now and again to rage against its captivity and rack its mind with a thousand schemes—and searching, searching, always searching! Searching for telepathic contact with creatures capable of operating the locks of its prison. And now, waking after its last fifty year trance, finding them!"

He nodded and caught her trembling hands in his.

"Look," he said, "do you know where the creature's prison is located?"

She glanced up at him fearfully. "Oh, yes, it printed the coordinates of the place on my mind as if my brain were graph paper. You see, the creature has a kind of colorless perception that lets it see out of its prison. It sees through rock as it sees through air and what it sees it measures. I'm sure that it knows all about Earth—because it knows exactly what it wants to do with Earth, beginning with the forced evolution of new dominant life forms from the insects and arachnids . . . and other organisms whose sensation-tone pleases it more than that of the mammals."

He nodded again. "All right," he said, "that pretty well settles what you and I have got to do. Dean and Hobart and Evelyn are under its control—we've got to suppose that. It may detach one or even two of them for the side job of finishing us off, just as it tried to use you to finish me. But it's a dead certainty that it's guiding at least one of them as fast as is humanly possible to its prison, to release it. We can't call in Interplanetary Police or look for help anywhere. Everything hinges on our being telepathic, and it would take days to convince them even of that. We've got to handle this all by ourselves. There's not a soul in the world can help us. We've got to hire an all-purpose flyabout that can make the trip, and we've got to go down there. While you were unconscious I put through some calls. Evelyn has left the office. She hasn't gone home. Hobart should be at his laboratory, but he isn't. Dean's home station can't get in touch with him. We can't hope to intercept them on the way— I thought of getting I.P. to nab them by inventing some charges against them, but that would probably end with the police stopping *us*. The only place where we have a chance of finding them, and of stopping them, is down there, where *it* is.

"And we'll have to be ready to kill them."

For millenniums piled on millenniums, the gales of Earth's loftiest, coldest, loneliest continent had driven the powdered ice against the dull metal without scoring it, without rusting it, without even polishing it. Like some grim temple sacred to pitiless gods it rose from the Antarctic gorge, a blunt hemisphere ridged with steps, with a tilted platform at the top, as if for an altar. A temple built to outlast eternity. Unmistakably the impression came through that this structure was older than Earth, older perhaps than the low-circling sun, that it had felt colds to which this was summer warmth, that it had known the grip of forces to which these ice-fisted gales were playful breezes, that it had known loneliness to which this white wasteland was teeming with life.

Not so the two tiny figures struggling toward it from one of three flyabouts lying crazily atilt on the drift. Their every movement betrayed frail humanity. They stumbled and swayed, leaning into the wind. Sometimes a gust would send them staggering. Sometimes one would fall. But always they came on. Though their clothing appeared roughly adequate—the sort of polar clothing a person might snatch up in five minutes in the temperate zone— it was obvious that they could not survive long in this frigid region. But that did not seem to trouble them.

Behind them toiled two other tiny figures, coming from the second grounded flyabout. Slowly, very slowly, they gained on the first two. Then a fifth figure came from behind a drift and confronted the second pair.

"Steady now. Steady!" Dean Horn shouted against the wind, leveling his blaster. "Mort! Grayl! For your lives, don't move!"

For a moment these words resounded in Mort's ears with the inhuman and mocking finality of the Antarctic gale. Then the faintly hopeful thought came to him that Dean would hardly have spoken that way if he had been under the creature's control. He would hardly have bothered to speak at all.

The wind shrieked and tore. Mort staggered and threw an arm around Grayl's shoulders for mutual support.

Dean fought his way toward them, blaster always leveled. In his other hand he had a small black cube—his static box, Mort recognized. He held it a little in front of him (like a cross, Mort thought) and as he came close to them he thrust it toward their heads (as if he were exorcising demons, Mort thought). Only then did Dean lower the muzzle of his blaster.

143

Mort said, "I'm glad you didn't count lurching with the wind as moving."

Dean smiled harshly. "I dodged the thing, too," he explained. "Just managed to flick on my static box. Like you did, I guess. Only I had no way of knowing that, so when I saw you I had to make sure I—"

The circular beam of a blaster hissed into the drift beside them, raining a great cloud of steam and making a hole wide as a bushel basket. Mort lunged at Dean, toppling him down out of range, pulling Grayl after.

"Hobart and Evelyn!" He pointed. "In the hollow ahead! Blast to keep them in it, Dean. What I've got in mind won't take long. Grayl, stay close to Dean . . . and give me your static box!"

He crawled forward along a curve that would take him to the edge of the hollow. Behind him and at the further side of the hollow, snow puffed into clouds of steam as the blasters spat free energy. Finally he glimpsed a shoulder, cap, and upturned collar. He estimated the distance, hefted Grayl's static box, guessed at the wind and made a measured throw. Blaster-fire from the hollow ceased. He rushed forward, waving to Dean and Grayl.

Hobart was sitting in the snow, staring dazedly at the weapon in his hand, as if it could tell him why he'd done what he'd done. He looked up at Mort with foggy eyes. The black static box had lodged in the collar of his coat and Mort felt a surge of confidence at the freakish accuracy of his toss.

But Evelyn was nowhere in sight. Over the lip of the hollow, very close now, appeared the ridged and dully gleaming hemisphere, like the ascendant disk of some tiny and ill-boding asteroid. A coldness that was more than that of the ice-edged wind went through Mort. He snatched

Hobart's blaster and ran. The other shouted after him, but he only waved back at them once, frantically.

The metal of the steps seemed to suck warmth even from the wind that ripped at his back like a snow-tiger as he climbed. The steps were as crazily tilted as those in a nightmare, and there seemed always to be more of them, as if they were somehow growing and multiplying. He found himself wondering if material and mental steps could ever get mixed.

He reached the platform. As his head came up over the edge, he saw, hardly a dozen feet away, Evelyn's face, blue with cold but having frozen into the same spiderish expression he had once seen in Grayl's. He raised the blaster, but in the same moment the face dropped out of sight. There was a metallic clang. He scrambled up onto the platform and clawed impotently at the circular plate barring the opening into which Evelyn had vanished. He was still crouched there when the others joined him.

The demon wind had died, as if it were the Mind Spider's ally and had done its work. The hush was like a prelude to a planet's end, and Hobart's bleak words, gasped out disjointedly, were like the sentence of doom.

"There are two doors. The thing told us all about them . . . while we were under its control. The first would be open . . . we were to go inside and shut it behind us. That's what Evelyn's done . . . she's locked it from the inside . . . just the simplest sliding bolt . . . but it will keep us from getting at her . . . while she activates the locks of the second door . . . the real door. We weren't to get the instructions . . . on how to do that . . . until we got inside."

"Stand aside," Dean said, aiming his blaster at the trapdoor, but he said it dully, as if he knew beforehand that it wasn't going to work. Waves of heat made the white hill beyond them waver. But the dull metal did not change color and when Dean cut off his blaster and tossed down a handful of snow on the spot, it did not melt.

Mort found himself wondering if you could make a metal of frozen thought. Through his numbed mind flashed a panorama of the rich lands and seas of the Global Democracy they had flown over yesterday—the green-framed white powder stations of the Orinoco, the fabulous walking cities of the Amazon Basin, the jet-atomic launching fields of the Gran Chaco, the multi-domed Oceanographic Institute of the Falkland Islands. A dawn world, you might call it. He wondered vaguely if other dawn worlds had struggled an hour or two into the morning only to fall prey to thinks like the Mind Spider.

"No!" The word came like a command heard in a dream. He looked up dully and realized that it was Grayl who had spoken—realized, with stupid amazement, that her eyes were flashing with anger.

"No! There's still one way we can get at it and try to stop it. The same way it got at us. Thought! It took us by surprise. We didn't have time to prepare resistance. We were panicked and it's given us a permanent panic-psychology. We could only think of getting behind our thought-screens and about how—once there—we'd never dare come out again. Maybe this time, if we all stand firm when we open our screens . . .

"I know it's a slim chance, a crazy chance . . ."

Mort knew that too. So did Dean and Hobart. But something in him, and in them, rejoiced at Grayl's words, rejoiced at the prospect of meeting the thing, however hopelessly, on it's own ground, mind to mind. Without hesitation they brought out their static boxes, and, at the signal of Dean's hand uplifted, switched them off.

That action plunged them from a material wilderness of snow and bleakly clouded sky into a sunless, dimensionless wilderness of thought. Like some lone fortress on an endless plain, their minds linked together, foursquare, waiting the assault. And like some monster of nightmare, the thoughts of the creature that accepted the name of the Mind Spider rushed toward them across that plain, threatening to overmaster them by the Satanic prestige that absolute selfishness and utter cruelty confer. The brassy stench of its being was like a poison cloud.

They held firm. The thoughts of the Mind Spider darted about, seeking a weak point, then seemed to settle down upon them everywhere, engulfingly, like a dry black web.

Alien against human, egocentric killer-mind against mutually loyal preserver-minds—and in the end it was the mutual loyalty and knittedness that turned the tide, giving them each a four-fold power of resistance. The thoughts of the Mind Spider retreated. Theirs pressed after. They sensed that a corner of his mind was not truly his. They pressed a pincers attack at that point, seeking to cut it off. There was a moment of desperate resistance. Then suddenly they were no longer four minds against the Spider, but five.

The trapdoor opened. It was Evelyn. They could at last switch on their thought-screens and find refuge behind the walls of neutral gray and prepare to fight back to their flyabouts and save their bodies.

But there was something that had to be said first, something that Mort said for them.

"The danger remains and we probably can't ever destroy it. *They* couldn't destroy it, or they wouldn't have built this prison. We can't tell anyone about it. Non-telepaths wouldn't believe all our story and would want to find out what was inside. We Horns have the job of being a monster's jailers. Maybe someday we'll be able to practice telepathy again—behind some sort of static-spheres. We will have to prepare for that time and work out many precautions, such as keying our static boxes, so that switching on one switches on all. But the Mind Spider and its prison remains our responsibility and our trust, forever."

# SAMUEL R. DELANY

*04594 Babel 17 $1.50

19683 Einstein Intersection $1.50

20571 The Ballad of Beta2/Empire Star $1.25

22642 The Fall of the Towers $1.95

39021 Jewels of Aptor 75¢

# ROGER ZELAZNY

37468 Isle of the Dead $1.50

16704 The Dream Master $1.50

24903 Four For Tomorrow $1.50

80694 This Immortal $1.50

# PHILIP JOSÉ FARMER

05360 Behind the Walls of Terra $1.25

78652 The Stone God Awakens $1.25

89238 The Wind Whales of Ishmael $1.25

*Available wherever paperbacks are sold or use this coupon.*

**FRITZ LEIBER**

| | | |
|---|---|---|
| 06218 | The Big Time | $1.25 |
| 30301 | Green Millennium | $1.25 |
| 53330 | Mindspider | $1.50 |
| 76110 | Ships to the Stars | $1.50 |
| 79152 | Swords Against Death | $1.25 |
| 79173 | Swords and Deviltry | $1.50 |
| 79162 | Swords Against Wizardry $1.25 | |
| 79182 | Swords in the Mist | $1.25 |
| 79222 | The Swords of Lankhmar $1.25 | |
| 95146 | You're All Alone | 95¢ |